I KNOW WHAT I SAW

K.T. CARLISLE

Copyright © 2025 by K.T. Carlisle

All rights reserved.

No part of this publication may be reproduced, distributed, or transmitted in any form or by any means, including photocopying, recording, or other electronic or mechanical methods, without the prior written permission of the publisher, except as permitted by U.S. copyright law. For permission requests, contact ktcarlisle15@gmail.com.

The story, all names, characters, and incidents portrayed in this production are fictitious. No identification with actual persons (living or deceased), places, buildings, and products is intended or should be inferred.

Book Cover by K.T. Carlisle, photo credit Autumn Kauffer

CONTENTS

Chapter 1	1
Chapter 2	5
Chapter 3	21
Chapter 4	31
Chapter 5	43
Chapter 6	53
Chapter 7	61
Chapter 8	73
Chapter 9	95
Chapter 10	109
Chapter 11	123
Chapter 12	135
Chapter 13	143
Chapter 14	157
Chapter 15	169

Chapter 16	181
Chapter 17	189
Chapter 18	207
Chapter 19	217
Chapter 20	225
Chapter 21	235
Chapter 22	247
Chapter 23	271
Chapter 24	287
Chapter 25	297
Chapter 26	309
Chapter 27	317

For the Village of Whitehall, NY, and all of its wonderfully wild inhabitants.

This book would not exist without you.

Chapter 1

I had that dream again last night. The one where I die at the end. Some people say it's not possible to dream about your death—especially not seventeen-year-old girls with their entire lives ahead of them—but I do. I have for years. But lately, the dreams have been coming more frequently. Like they used to after it first happened. The thing I try not to think about but can never forget. Maybe it's just a coincidence, but I can't shake the feeling that it means more than that. Like a warning.

Something is coming.

The dream always starts the same. I get into the passenger seat of a car I don't recognize. I strain my eyes to find who's driving, but all I see is the silhouette of a figure that seems too big to fit inside the cramped cabin of the small sedan. Its head hunches over the dashboard, arms thick as tree branches bent at awkward angles, hands like baseball mitts gripping the steering wheel tight. The forest whips by the car windows as we speed down winding dirt roads deeper into the night. The faster we go, the harder my heart thumps against my ribcage until all I can hear is the thrum of my blood rushing past my ears as the fear and adrenaline course through my veins.

Suddenly, the sound of my cell phone pierces through the silence in the car like a hunting knife tearing through flesh. I reach inside my pocket to retrieve the phone, a serpent of fear coiling in my intestines as I anticipate what the reaction will be from my faceless chauffeur.

"Hello?"

The moment the word leaves my lips, I smother a scream as the driver turns its massive head to face me for the first time. I still can't distinguish its features through the inky black shadows surrounding us, but what I see is enough to bring the rushing in my ears to a screeching halt. A pair of glowing red eyes are staring back at me, watching me with such intensity, I can almost feel them pressing against my skin. Just as I find the courage to open my mouth and release the shriek I've been stifling, I hear a voice come through the phone, gravelly and demonic as it reaches my ear.

"*I want you to run*," it tells me. "*Run, Eliza!*"

But I can't run. The creature in the driver's seat is trained on me. Watching. Daring me to make a move. I reach for the door handle, but it's too late. In a flash, the beast uncurls its long, spiderlike fingers from the steering wheel, a glint of moonlight catching in its razor-sharp claws right before it thrusts them into my abdomen. My mouth fills with the taste of metal, vision blackens at the edges, the tunnel growing darker, more pronounced as the monster tears apart my guts. Right before I slip into death's cold embrace, I hear this horrible, unearthly sound, like a cross between an ambulance and a howler monkey whooping through the night air.

That's when I wake up.

It's only a dream, I reassure myself. And I know it's the truth. Still, every time I hear that voice, see those eyes, feel that *thing* tearing into me, I'm reminded of that night. The one night I wish more than anything I could take back. The one night I want more than anything to forget. But I can't. I'll *never* forget it. Because I know what I saw.

And no one believes me.

Chapter 2

It's always so much harder to pry myself out of bed after spending the entire night trying to escape the clutches of a monster that nobody else believes in. But it's even more difficult knowing that the only thing I have to look forward to is another miserable day at Whitehall High. I wonder whether I'll get body-checked into a locker today or how many spitballs I'll have to comb out of my hair between classes. Maybe I just won't go at all. Maybe I'll stay in bed all day instead. Maybe I'll—

"E? You up yet, sweetheart?" Dad's gentle voice creeps in through the crack in my bedroom door from his place in the hallway. It feels good to hear him call me by my preferred nickname; it reminds me that I'm no longer trapped in that awful nightmare. After all, nobody calls me Eliza aside from my teachers. Anyone who I consider a friend or family member calls me E, which pretty much only covers two people in the entire universe. It used to be more. I used to have a lot of friends back in middle school.

But that was before everything changed.

Dad knows how much I value my privacy, so he waits until I tell him it's okay, I'm decent before entering my bedroom. "It's almost time for school," he tells me like I don't already know. Like I haven't been dreading it since the moment I woke up. "If you don't leave soon, you're gonna be late. Time to get a move on, Little Foot."

He grabs one of my toes through the puffy, white duvet still covering my body on the bed and I squirm out of his grasp.

"*Dad!*" I whine like the mortified teenager I am. "God, you are so *embarrassing!* I'm up, okay? Now, get out of here so I can get dressed."

I rip the covers off and jump out of bed, shoving my smirking father out the door and locking it behind him. The floorboards of our old two-story farmhouse creak as he wanders down the hallway, his footsteps falling with heavy thuds as he continues down the staircase to the kitchen.

"Better get changed quick," he warns, "or I'll give your breakfast to Riley!"

The geriatric Coonhound gives a throaty howl at the sound of her name. I imagine her long tail thumping against the couch cushions from her place on the lumpy sofa in front of the bay windows in our living room that overlook the quiet suburb beyond. There was a time when she'd be curled up at the foot of my bed, protecting me from Dad's grabby games, but she's old now, and her weary joints can't carry her up the stairs like they once could. So, she's resigned to the life of a couch potato.

I amble over to my dresser and pull the first change of clothes I can find out of the top drawer: a pair of ripped, black skinny jeans, and a Black Sabbath tee shirt with the band's name written in purple bubble letters across the front. It's probably not considered "cool" to listen to heavy metal bands from the 60s, but whatever. I like them. Besides, it wouldn't matter if I were sporting a tee with the latest Taylor Swift album printed across the fabric. Everyone at school would still hate my guts.

Once I'm dressed, I head next door to the bathroom to brush my teeth and drag a comb through my hair. The light from the sconces above the mirror struggles to find its way out from beneath the frosted glass surrounding each bulb, falling muted against the yellowed, floral wallpaper that Dad promises to replace but never does. Other girls would complain that it's not bright enough in here for them to do their hair and makeup, but I don't mind. I don't spend much time in front of the mirror anyway. It's too painful. Not because I think I'm ugly, but if I stare at my reflection for too long, I start to see my mom. I've got the same pointed nose, the same gray-blue eyes, the same thin lips that used to shower me with kisses before the cancer came and took that all away forever.

I keep my gaze on the porcelain sink basin, taking a quick peek in the faded mirror just to make sure I don't have any toothpaste smeared in the corner of my mouth or (God forbid) a pimple on my nose. The last thing I need is to give the hyenas at school another reason to laugh at me. Aside from the fact that the streaks in my hair are looking more pastel than shocking pink, I look presentable enough. Not that anyone cares. No one looks at me anyway.

Before I head downstairs, I duck into my room one last time to grab my backpack off the back of my desk chair and my cell phone from its place on my nightstand. My breath catches in my throat when I realize what time it is.

Dang it!

I wasted too much time in bed this morning thinking about that stupid nightmare. There's only twenty minutes until first period, which gives me just enough time to drive to Whitehall High, park the car, and stop by my locker with five minutes to spare—but only if I leave right now. Looks like Riley is going to be scarfing down my breakfast after all. Lucky girl.

I race down the stairs as fast as my feet will carry me without tripping. The smell of bacon and maple syrup smacks me in the face as soon as I hit the first-floor landing, the delicious aroma making my stomach cry out in anger that I spent so much time moping in bed.

"Sorry, Dad," I groan as I round the corner from the staircase into the kitchen. "No time to sit and eat today. I got a late start."

He twists his head over his broad shoulders and gives me a wink, the crow's feet around his green eyes crinkling as he does so. As he turns away from the laminated countertop, I can see a hunk of tinfoil in his hand, which he extends to me.

"Made ya a bacon, egg, and cheese for the road," he says, the calluses on his hands rough against my scalp as he tousles my hair and attempts to bring me in for a bear hug. Before he can swallow me in his powerful arms, I place my hand on his chest and give him a scrutinizing stare.

"Did you remember to—?"

"Yes, yes, I remembered the maple syrup," he chuckles. "What? You think I don't know my own daughter by now?"

He wraps his arms around me as I soften, not fighting the affection as hard as I normally would, feeling too grateful to play the role of moody teenager.

"Thanks, Dad," I mumble into his flannel shirt as he holds me to his chest.

"No problem, Little Foot." I can hear the smile in his voice as he says the nickname that he knows I hate. Almost as much as I hate being called *Liza*.

"And you ruined it," I announce, pushing away from him with the sandwich clutched in my hand as I make my way to the front door and begin lacing up my Converse sneakers. I make sure to smile at him to let him know I'm joking. Sort of.

"Don't forget I need your help at the store after school," he reminds me as I bolt out the door, down the front porch, and into the front seat of Mom's old Beetle. I assure him I'll be there before closing the driver's side door and bringing the car to life. With the mid-September chill settling in the engine, it takes three tries to get it started, and Dad watches from the porch to make sure I'm alright. I give him the thumbs up to let him know everything's okay and before I know it, I'm puttering down the cracked asphalt of our rundown little street.

As I panic drive to my doom, I can't help but notice how beautiful Whitehall is this time of year. Even on sunny days like today, there's a low-hanging fog that creeps over the Champlain Canal, which once was home to a bustling shipyard where colonists built the first naval fleets to fight off the British soldiers. The Adirondacks are dotted with red and orange with changing leaves as the autumnal air sweeps through the region, making the mountains look like they're on fire. Most of the neighborhoods are shabby, with narrow, two-story farmhouses just like mine that were built way back in the early 1900s and reek of neglect. But once you get to the main village where the richer folks live, it's all Victorian glamor and white-steepled churches that look like something straight out of a New England postcard. Maybe that's why Whitehall is nicknamed The Smallest Town in New York. Either that or the population of less than four thousand people—a number that's only decreased in recent years. If I didn't know any better, I'd never guess that there was something amiss hiding between the tall pines and towering oaks that surround our little hamlet.

But I do know better.

I pull into the parking lot of Whitehall High, careful to divert my eyes away from the woods that surround the schoolyard. There are fifteen minutes left until first period. I snatch the sandwich Dad made me and my backpack off the passenger's seat, slinging it over my shoulder as I race to the school's front entrance. It's a blocky brick building that looks more like a prison than a high school (like there's a difference between the two). As I enter through the double glass doors, the image of a navy-colored ship is etched into the white-painted cinderblock walls with the inscription, *Whitehall Vikings*. Before I can even get my bearings, someone intentionally walks into me, sending my sandwich tumbling to the linoleum.

"Watch it, Liza Lot," Brittany Wheeler sneers at me as she continues down the hallway. Her auburn hair bounces behind her from her high ponytail as she leaves me standing there with my heart in my throat and the sound of that stupid nickname ringing in my ears.

Liza.

I'll admit, it doesn't sound like much of an insult. Not until you understand its real meaning, at least. I was born Eliza Jane Lee-Loft on August 2, 2006. It's a mouthful, I know, but the "Lee" got dropped after Mom had a falling out with Grandma over something that was "none of my business" and she promised to tell me all about once I was "old enough." She never got the chance, though. Breast cancer sucks. Whatever. I don't want to talk about it.

But sometimes I wish she had lived long enough to at least tell me why she abandoned her maiden name. It's not just the fact that I miss her like crazy and I don't have much to remember her by (aside from her beat-up old Volkswagen Beetle that I somehow manage to drive around town even though it's in desperate need of new tires... and starter... and transmission). It's the fact that without the "Lee" there, it became that much easier for the kids at school to tease me. Liza Lee-Loft sounds like a fearsome cowgirl straight out of a spaghetti western, complete with a ten-gallon hat and sharp-shootin' pistols tucked away on either side of her hips that never miss their mark. No one would ever mess with *her*. But Liza Loft? She's nothing but a wimpy loser full of tall tales and wild conspiracy theories about cryptids hiding out in the woods. You can't be afraid of a girl like Liza, much less trust a word she says. After all, Liza lies. A lot.

Liza Loft. Lies a lot. Now, do you get it?

It's lame, and I know I shouldn't let it bother me as much as it does, but when I hear Brittany use that lousy anagram on me, all I want to do is make her feel as small and insignificant as I do. But before I can come up with a retort, a bony arm slings around my shoulders and all the anger melts away.

"Yeah, keep walkin'!" My newfound companion calls after her, but only once the bully is safely out of earshot. I don't mind that his bravery is masked by cowardice. It's just nice to have a friend in a sea of foes, and friends don't get much better than Simon Little.

"Thanks, Si," I smile, tucking my hair behind my ear as he scoops up the sandwich I dropped and hands it back to me. The heat in my chest subsides and is replaced with the warmth that only true friendship can provide. He waves away my gratitude with a swipe of his scrawny hand, which he then uses to push his thick-framed glasses up the bridge of his hook nose.

"Don't mention it," he says. We traverse the halls together, winding through the disparate cliques of students still gathered in clumps beside their lockers, not yet ready to resign themselves to the confines of the classrooms that await them. Eventually, we arrive at my locker, and Simon leans off to the side while I swap out the textbooks in my bag for the ones I'll need for my first few classes of the day.

"What took you so long anyway?" he asks. "Was starting to think you weren't coming in today."

"I just... got a late start is all," I lie. It's not that I don't trust Simon. I've told him about my nightmare before. But I'm just not in the mood to hear his wild theories about what it all means. Once he gets going, there's no telling when (or if) he'll ever stop.

Lucky for me, Simon doesn't detect the subtle notes of dishonesty in my voice. Or if he does, he doesn't say anything about it. Instead, he leans in conspiratorially, his dark eyebrows raised high above his deep brown eyes as he stares at me.

"Did you hear what they found out by Saranac Lake?" I pause at the question, my fingertips hovering above the science textbook I need for first period.

"Do I want to know?"

"Probably not," he snickers, "but you know I'm gonna tell you anyway."

"Okay, but hurry up," I tell him. "The bell's gonna ring any minute, and if I'm late to first period again, Mrs. Morton is gonna kill me."

"You can't rush a good story," Simon teases me with a smirk. I give him a sharp look that straightens his spine in an instant. He puts up his hands in defense.

"Okay, okay, I'll give you the short version: They found a body out in the woods."

A shiver trails from the base of my neck down to my tailbone. *Not again.*

"When did this happen?" I'm surprised at how even my voice sounds. It almost convinces me that I'm not afraid. I'm not panicking.

"Mid-August, I think," Simon says. "It didn't show up on my list at first. I think they were trying to cover it up, y'know? But they had a press release about it on Friday. It's been making the rounds in the community all weekend. I'm surprised you didn't hear about it."

I don't need to guess what Simon means when he refers to "the community." I know he's not talking about the residents of Whitehall or our classmates. He's talking about people like us.

He's talking about believers.

"I needed a break this weekend," I admit. The statement hangs heavy in the air. I can almost feel the wrinkled flesh of the elephant-sized words left unspoken. Tears prickle at the back of my eyes and I have to swallow the lump in my throat to keep from breaking down.

Not here. Not now.

Simon places a gentle hand on my shoulder, and I have to hide my face to keep him from seeing the single tear that slides down my cheek.

"I'm sorry." He grimaces. "That was stupid. I should've realized. I—"

"It's okay." I brush it off, brush the tears away, suck in a deep breath, and paste on a smile before turning back to him. "Now, tell me more about this body in the woods."

Better to focus on someone else's tragedy than wallow over Mom's deathaversary, I think.

"Right." Simon straightens up again, the excitement returning to his eyes. He launches into an explanation of the gruesome discovery made just two hours north of our little town. "At first, they called it a hiking accident—*a hiking accident*, can you believe that? But that's *not* what happened. I'm telling you right now. Something is *up!*"

"Tick tock, Si," I remind him, my patience wearing as thin as the crowd of students depositing themselves into their first-period classrooms. Simon kicks it into high gear.

"It was a girl—one of the campers at the grounds or something—and when they found her, she was torn apart so bad, they almost couldn't identify her."

My heart sinks like a stone in the pit of my stomach as I shove the last of my textbooks into my backpack and slam the locker door shut. I start cycling through the follow-up questions that I'm certain Simon has already considered. He wouldn't have brought it up at all if he hadn't, but I have to ask. It's routine.

"Arms and legs?"

"Completely removed," he confirms as we make our way to the end of the hall.

"Witnesses?"

"Negative."

"Footprints?"

"Nothing 'official'—" Simon rolls his eyes as he places the word in air quotes, "—but when have they ever included *that* in the report? A local did snap a pretty convincing photo, though, and uploaded it to the board over the weekend. I think it's legit."

I nod, hesitating over the last question I don't want to ask but have to. Finally, it leaves my lips as we reach the end of the hallway.

"Sightings?"

"Multiple." Simon's eyes widen, impressing the significance of his response on me. We don't say it out loud, but we're both thinking the same thing. He lowers his voice before speaking again, "We might be able to get one of them to be on the show at the festival."

The festival. With all the sadness over the weekend and the strangeness of my nightmare, I almost forgot all about it. But Simon's reminder is all it takes for the butterflies in my stomach to start flapping their nervous wings. He sees the apprehension written all over my face and nudges me on the shoulder.

"Don't give me that look," he teases. "It's gonna be *fun!* Just think about it: Our first-ever live show at the biggest gathering of Bigfoot enthusiasts on the East Coast!"

"Shh!" I hiss, clamping my hand over his mouth as I dart my head over my shoulder to make sure no one heard. "Keep your voice down."

I feel the grin spread across his lips beneath my palm before I tear my hand away from his face and he laughs at my mortified expression. Before I can say another word, the bell to first period rings.

"*Simon!*" My eyes flash with anger as I smack him on the shoulder. "You made me late, you jerk."

He rubs his shoulder for dramatic effect, milking his non-injury for all it's worth as he walks backward down the hallway in the opposite direction toward his first class of the day.

"Sorry, E!" he calls out to me. "See you in English!"

As he turns his back to me, I can see the unmistakable white silhouette of a Sasquatch printed across the back of his black tee shirt. Beneath it is the tagline, "Whitehall, NY: Bigfoot Capitol of the Northeast." The words seem to mock me as I watch him disappear through the door to his classroom. I let out a frustrated grunt and turn toward Mrs. Morton's class, trying not to think about the dead girl in Saranac Lake. Trying even harder not to think about my encounter and what happened to Renée Pope all those years ago.

It's not connected. It can't be connected.

But somehow, I know it is. And it terrifies me.

Chapter 3

Mrs. Morton takes it easy on me for walking into class late. I think she feels a little sorry for me. In a small town like Whitehall, everyone knows everything about everybody else (or at least, they try to), so she probably assumes my tardiness has something to do with my mom's death. Normally, the special treatment would bother me. It's bad enough that people think I'm a nutcase; I don't need them treating me like I'm some sort of emotional trainwreck on top of it. But I'm grateful for Mrs. Morton's lenience. I don't have the energy to deal with a teacher's wrath. Not after the morning I've had.

Not after what Simon told me.

My first few classes go by in a blur. I hardly register the lecture on Newton's laws of physics that Mrs. Morton spouts off in her mind-numbing monotone. Mr. Phillips's oration on civil rights and liberties goes right over my head so by the time his class on American Government concludes, I feel as though I've learned nothing. Thankfully, Madame Sage is out sick today, so I don't have to fake my way through French class. I just hope there's not a pop quiz on the screening of *Molière* she left the sub with or I can kiss my B+ average *au revoir*. It seems the only things my mind is willing to focus on this morning are those glowing red eyes from my nightmare, that mangled body up in Saranac, and the shadowy memories of that night in the woods. What I saw.

What I did.

I'm so wrapped up in my thoughts that I don't even have time to mentally prepare myself before walking into Mr. Atkins's pre-calculus class. So, when my eyes land on the couple making out by the lockers outside his classroom door, I can't stop myself from staring. Can't stop the color as it drains from my cheeks. Can't keep my stomach from dropping to my feet. I want to throw up, and it's not just because the smack of saliva coming from their hungry lips sends this weird, tingly feeling spiraling in my gut. It's because I'd give anything to trade places with the pretty blonde cheerleader pressed against the locker. To feel Joel Baker's hands sliding down my back as he slips his tongue inside my mouth. To run my fingers through his thick, brown curls. Feel the leather sleeves of his letterman jacket as he holds me tight.

Jealousy is such an ugly feeling. It makes me feel dirty, like when Dad used to take me out camping on West Mountain when I was a kid and we couldn't shower until we got back home. But I can't help it. Because deep down, I know it could have been me on the receiving end of Joel's kisses—not Carissa King. After all, she and I used to be best friends. We used to rule the school together. But not anymore. Not since—

"Gross, perv!" Carissa's blue eyes fixate on me as she pulls away for air and I feel the color return to my face, flushing my cheeks scarlet. Joel follows her gaze past his shoulder and sees me staring, the discovery curling the corners of his mouth in a sneer. *Please, God, kill me now.*

"C'mon, ladies." Mr. Atkins's voice rescues me from the moment, but I can still feel my skin burning with embarrassment. "Class is about to start. Get to your seats."

Carissa untangles herself from her boyfriend—the boyfriend that should be mine, the boyfriend that I can only dream of having no thanks to her—but not before making a show of planting a juicy kiss on his lips. I dart into the room without another glance in their direction, slinking into my desk before folding my arms across the surface and sinking my head on top.

Stupid, stupid, stupid! Can this day possibly get any worse? As if responding to my unspoken question, I feel a spitball ping against the back of my head and the whole class bursts into laughter. I dig my fingers through my hair to find the soggy culprit and flick it to the floor without picking my head up. Through the commotion, I hear Carissa's nasally voice greet her best friend. The third member of what used to be our inseparable trio.

"Oh em *gee*, Kate, you will not be-*lieve* what just happened," Carissa cackles.

"Tell me *everything*," Kate gushes. I can almost see the sheen of saliva frothing over her thick, pink lips as she waits for a fresh dose of hot goss from her queen bee, but I don't confirm it. I'm happy to pretend that I'm invisible.

"That perverted little *freak* over there was just watching me and Joel. She couldn't get enough of it! I thought she was gonna whip out her phone and start taking pictures or something. Totally disgusting."

That's it.

"Hey!" I snap my head in their direction before I can stop myself, indignation radiating through every inch of my body. Then I say something even more stupid, "Shut up, okay?"

"Ex-*cuse* me?" Carissa balks, the nostrils flaring around her dainty nose.

"Oohh, now you're gonna get it," Kate warns. A malevolent twinkle flashes across her hazel eyes as she anticipates Carissa's next move. She props her elbows up on her desk and rests her head in her hands, her caramel-colored skin smooth and serene as she takes in the scene. Like this is a movie, and I'm everyone's least-favorite character about to get written out of the script with a serious butt-kicking.

Crap. Why did I say that? My mouth goes dry. I can taste bile biting at the back of my throat. Everyone is staring at me, waiting for me to say something back. To come to my own defense. Part of me wants to back down, retract my statement, pretend it never happened. But it's too late for that now. So, instead, I double down.

"Just leave me alone," I grumble.

"Or what?" Carissa snipes back.

"Yeah, *Liza*. Or what?" Kate parrots. They leer at me from across the room, their eyes taunting. Willing me to respond. But they already know the answer. They know as well as I do that there's nothing I can say or do that will hurt them. Just like they know that I know that they'd never do anything to cause me any real harm. We have history. And like it or not, that history binds us together. Otherwise, we'd all be in trouble.

Big trouble.

The bell rings and the tension dissipates as Mr. Atkins closes the door and takes his place at the front of the room. I twist around in my seat without another word to Carissa or Kate, but I can still feel their eyes shooting daggers into the back of my skull for the rest of the class.

It's hard enough to focus on pre-calculus on an uneventful day what with Mr. Atkins being the teacher. He's not boring or anything. Quite the opposite. With his jokey, lighthearted charm, he manages to make a dry subject like pre-calculus fun and engaging. But add that to the fact that he's a total heartthrob, and it's easy to understand why most girls need to take him up on the offer of after-school tutoring. I get it. My heart is set on Joel, but I'm not blind. Even I sometimes get too caught up in the sight of his dreamy, sky-blue eyes and dimpled cheeks to retain any information. The combination of his good looks and my showdown with Carissa and Kate makes it impossible to pay attention at all. It's a relief when the bell finally rings, and it's time to move on to my next class. Even more of a relief when I realize that the next class is English.

As I stand to leave, my eyes lock with Carissa's. She's not finished with me. Not by a long shot. I scramble to throw my textbook in my bag so I can high-tail it out of there before she has time to hurl more insults my way. But it turns out, I don't need to hurry. Once again, Mr. Atkins steps in to save the day.

"Carissa," he calls out from his desk. "Can you stay behind a moment? I need to speak with you."

I don't join the chorus of *ooooh's* that erupts around me, but I'd be lying if I said I didn't leave the room with a smile on my face. *Serves her right.* With Carissa tied up with Mr. Atkins and Kate no doubt lingering behind like the obedient lackey she is, I'm free to head to English class without fear of another fight. I'm so relieved, I practically skip into Mrs. Sneider's classroom, taking the empty seat beside Simon, his copy of *Ethan Frome* already turned to the correct page. He's kind of a suck-up that way.

"You seem in better spirits," he comments, eyeing me with the slightest air of suspicion.

"Let's just say a certain someone finally got a little bit of karma thrown her way." I wink, and the gesture forces a mischievous grin across Simon's lips.

"Carissa?" he guesses.

"The one and only!"

"Spill."

Just as I'm about to fill Simon in on everything that happened in Mr. Atkins's class, the bell rings, and Mrs. Sneider demands our attention. She waddles to the front of the room, her pregnant belly like a giant water balloon ready to burst open at any moment.

"Okay, class, listen up!" She waits for her students to settle down, steadying herself against the ledge of the whiteboard as she takes the pressure off what I'm sure are aching, swollen feet stuffed inside her loafers. When the room is quiet, she rests a hand over her stomach and rubs it absent-mindedly as she speaks, "As you all know, I'm very, *very* pregnant. The baby is due next week, which means today will be my last day as your teacher. At least until the new year.

"Since I'll be gone for so long, you'll have a long-term sub in my place, and I want you all to be on your best behavior." There's a warning tone in her voice as she scans the room, her eyes lingering for a moment on Dave Truman and Tyler Jenkins—the class clowns in our midst. "I don't want to hear any reports of frogs hopping out of the teacher's desk or shaving cream inside his briefcase. Do I make myself clear, Mr. Truman? Mr. Jenkins? Any word of monkey business from either one of you two, and you're headed straight to the principal's office, understand?"

Dave and Tyler exchange amused glances with one another before answering in unison, "Yes, Mrs. Sneider."

"Perfect!" Mrs. Sneider claps her hands together and takes a step forward, her round cheeks rosy pink from the effort required to stand. She shuffles to the rolling chair behind her desk and takes a seat, unable to stifle the sigh of relief that escapes her lips as she does so. "Well, then," she breathes, "without any further ado, I'd like to introduce you to your new teacher, Mr. Pope."

With a wave of her hand, Mrs. Sneider gestures towards the back of the room and the blood in my veins frosts over. I can't help but cast a nervous glance at Simon. *Did he hear it, too?*

Sure enough, he's staring back at me, the astonishment in my eyes mirrored in his own.

"Did she just say, Mr. *Pope?*" he whispers. Before I can respond, a tall, muscular man strides to the front of the room, his hands shoved inside the pockets of his khakis, checkered button-down tucked neatly into his pants. He's young—probably in his mid-twenties, I would guess—with blonde hair that hangs low and scraggly over a pair of piercing green eyes that seem to darken when they land on me. When he speaks, I swear it's like we're the only two people in the room.

"I'm Mr. Pope," he announces. "Mrs. Sneider has told me so much about you, I feel like I know you already. But I'm really looking forward to getting to know you even better over the next few months."

I gulp around the golf ball lodged inside my throat. My palms begin to sweat. My legs feel like pool noodles drenched in chlorinated water. My heart is racing so fast, I worry that it might beat right out of my chest. Maybe it's just my imagination, or maybe it's my guilty conscience, but the way he's looking at me right now gives me the strangest feeling. Like he can see right inside my mind. Like he knows my secret.

That I saw what happened to his sister.

That I'm the reason she's dead.

Chapter 4

The bell above the general store's entrance chimes to signal my arrival as I push it open, but that doesn't stop Riley from letting out a deafening bray to let Dad know I'm here. She wobbles out from behind the wooden counter on the right where Dad is busy running through the inventory list. When she stops at my feet, I bend down and scratch the space between her ears, trying not to notice how her fur has lost its sheen and her skin has grown lumpy with fatty tumors and skin tags—a byproduct of her old age. Once upon a time, she and I used to run amuck around the shop, knocking candy bars and toothbrushes and fishing poles off the shelves depending on where our antics took us through the store. It used to drive Mom and Dad crazy. But Riley's too old for games now. We both are.

"Hey, E." Dad greets me from the counter. "How was school?"

Terrible, I think.

"Fine," I say instead.

"Learn anything interesting?"

Just that my new teacher is the brother of a dead girl who haunts my every thought.

"Not really," I tell him. What else can I say? I love my dad and we're probably closer than most teenage girls and their fathers—a loss like ours will do that, I guess—but not even Simon knows why Mr. Pope makes me so uneasy. I mean, he has *some* idea. After all, he was in the woods that night, too, and we both saw what happened to Renée. But he doesn't know what happened before that.

He doesn't know my secret.

"Can you grab a few boxes of ammo from the back, hon?" Dad changes the subject, and I couldn't be more grateful for the distraction.

"Sure thing," I say. "Any kind in particular?"

"Better make it the 12-gauge 5 shot. Can't believe it's turkey hunting season already." Dad shakes his head as if to say, *Where does the time go?* "Before you know it, we'll be celebrating Thanksgiving!"

"And before *you* know it, I'll be going away to college," I tease. Dad places a hand over his heart and staggers backward like my words are arrows and I've just shot him in the chest.

"Don't remind me," he groans with mock dread. But maybe it isn't a show. There's a wistful look in his eyes as he follows my movement from the front entrance through the door beside the counter that leads to the back of the shop where the inventory is kept.

Through the door is a cramped office the size of a closet on the left. It's hardly big enough to contain the ancient, boxy computer that's sat there ever since it was first purchased back in the early 2000s. I wouldn't be surprised if the decrepit device was included with the purchase of the store when my parents bought it after I was born. To the right is the storage area, which isn't that much bigger. Metal shelves line the wood-paneled walls on either side, stretching back only about ten feet before the narrow closet comes to a stop.

We don't keep much back here aside from toiletries and some of the more popular snacks that our regulars prefer—the things that tend to run out quicker than others. But there's also a stockpile of some of the less in-demand items that are harder to restock when supplies run low—like ghillie suits and live bait. And ammo. Outsiders—my Aunt Josie calls them Flatlanders, but that's just because she's from Vermont—they probably think it's strange that you can buy toilet paper and apply for your gun license all under one roof. But with the closest Walmart being twenty-six miles away, it's nice to have a place nearby where you can get all your shopping done in one go.

I try to stay focused on the task at hand, scanning through the boxes of ammo until I find the ones I need. I don't think about my nightmare. I don't think about Joel or Carissa or Kate. And I *definitely* don't think about Mr. Pope. Or what Simon wants us to do now that he's our new teacher.

"Forget the Saranac sightings," he said to me after class let out and we made our way to the cafeteria for lunch. "We can cover those on the podcast anytime. But an interview with *Asher Pope, live, at the Bigfoot Festival?* That would put us over the edge! Can you imagine what that would do for our show? We'd be overnight sensations! We might even outshine Robert Gimlin. Just think of it: A live interview with the brother of the victim of Whitehall's most infamous Bigfoot attack."

"Okay, let's not get carried away here." I tried to bring my friend back down to earth, but he already had his heart set on us making history in the cryptozoology community. "We don't even know if he's a believer. I mean, what if he buys into the official story? That Renée was murdered and her killer is still out there running free?"

Simon wasn't hearing any of it. As far as he was concerned, Asher Pope was going to be our guest on the podcast. And there was nothing I could say or do to dissuade him. Not without revealing what I couldn't let anyone know.

The ammo boxes are heavier than they look, so I can only manage to carry five at once before it becomes too awkward and I run the risk of spilling shells all over the floor. I balance them carefully in my hands and shuffle back out to the main shop, still trying to shake off the lingering memories of my miserable day at school. The shop probably isn't what most people think of when they imagine a convenience store. Rather than tiled linoleum floors and concrete walls, the place resembles more of a log cabin, with warm, wooden paneling throughout and creaky floorboards that remind me of the ones we have at home. We even have rocking chairs on the wraparound porch out front, which locals use to rest their tired feet during the summer after a long day swimming at Carver Falls or hiking the switchbacks at The Saddles State Forest.

I wind through the narrow shelves that line the open shop floor until I reach the place where the guns and ammo are stocked at the far end of the store. There's not much in the way of weaponry at our shop. Dad can't afford to hire an employee to man the gun counter full-time, which sometimes makes me feel a little guilty. Like maybe if I didn't have to go to school, I could help him more and he'd make bigger sales, and we wouldn't have to struggle so much to make ends meet. But for now, the small selection of pistols on display beneath the glass counter is enough to keep the lights on. Between the groceries we sell and the ammo we cycle through each hunting season, we do alright. I guess it could be worse.

It's a slow day at the store, so I pass the time doing homework behind the counter while Dad goes over every nook and cranny in the shop, checking and double-checking his inventory list to make sure it's accurate. When something is understocked, he asks me to grab it from the back. If we're running low, I let him know, and he makes a note to add it to the order when it's time to contact our supplier at the end of the month. I'm standing in the inventory closet grabbing a few bags of Doritos off the shelf when I hear the bell chime, alerting me to our first customer of the day. Or at least, the first one I've encountered since school ended.

"David," Dad announces in his cheerful 'customer service' voice. "It's good to see you!"

I peek through the door to spy who he's talking to before deciding it's safe to come out. If it's Dave Truman, I'd rather wait it out until he leaves than brave whatever tricks he has kept up his sleeves. I sigh with relief when I realize that it's not the incorrigible trickster from my English class at all. One look at the handsome, broad-shouldered blonde at the counter is all it takes for me to recognize that it's Mr. Atkins.

"Great to see you, too, Ed." He flashes a bright white smile at my dad and extends an open palm across the counter to shake his hand. I push through the door with the bags of chips in my arms. When Mr. Atkins's blue eyes meet mine, I politely wave and murmur a quiet hello before darting off to the snack aisle to deposit my bounty. I can feel his gaze follow me through the store, but I don't look back. I'm afraid he'll see the crimson creeping up my cheeks at his mere presence. He's even hotter outside of the classroom somehow.

"So, did you have a good summer off?" Dad resumes the conversation and I do my best to pretend like I'm not eavesdropping.

"Oh yeah, it was fine," Mr. Atkins responds. "Mostly just stayed up at the cabin for a bit and did some fishing. Nothing special."

"That the cabin your parents used to have way back when?" I sneak a peek over at the counter in time to see Mr. Atkins nodding his confirmation.

"Yeah, she's still in the family," he says like the cabin is a crazy aunt or a female cousin twice removed that he can't seem to get rid of. "Not quite the same as it used to be, but I don't mind roughing it a little. Besides, Saranac Lake is beautiful during the summer no matter where you happen to stay."

My heart skips a beat at the mention of Saranac Lake. Images of amputated limbs sprawled across the forest floor dance across my eyes, making it difficult to see. I reach out to steady my shaking nerves against the shelves and end up knocking an entire box of candy bars to the floor. *Idiot.*

As I scramble to the hardwood to pick up my mess, Mr. Atkins rushes to my aid, grabbing candy bars and popping them back inside their display box. My hands are trembling both from the mention of Saranac Lake and the sheer mortification of being the world's biggest klutz in front of the dreamiest teacher in school. I can feel my cheeks throbbing as they turn beet red when Mr. Atkins's fingertips graze the back of my hand as I reach for the last candy bar on the floor.

"Thanks, Mr. Atkins," I mumble, clutching the box of candy to my chest as I rise to stand. "You didn't have to do that."

"No trouble at all," he assures me. "And please—call me Dave. No need to be so formal when we're not at school."

He winks at me, and I swear to God, I can hear angels singing. If Mr. Atkins—excuse me, *Dave*—were Gaston, I'd be one of the blonde triplets in the corner of the marketplace swooning as he passes by while Belle croons out the lyrics of her opening number.

The moment passes before I can register whether it was real or imagined, and Mr. Atkins is back at the front counter.

"Guess I should be adding you to the payroll now," Dad quips when he approaches.

"Not unless you can match my current salary," Mr. Atkins jokes back. The two share a laugh while I hang back by the snack aisle for a minute longer, still too embarrassed to insert myself into the conversation.

"So, if I can't offer you a job, what can I do you for?" Dad asks.

"Well, I was hoping you might have one of those ghillie suits in stock," Mr. Atkins explains. "Mine got damaged, and I need a new one for the hunting season."

"Oh, yeah. We've got you covered. E, honey?" I reluctantly emerge from the snack aisle. "Can you grab Dave one of the ghillie suits from the back, please?"

I dart back to the inventory closet—actively avoiding eye contact with Mr. Atkins as I pass him on my way there—and return twenty seconds later with the suit. It's a weird getup, and even though I've seen the suits a thousand times, they never cease to give me the creeps. Probably because the long strands of sandy green imitation moss that drip down from the polyester material remind me too much of that night in the woods. That thing I saw. It's no wonder why Simon uses his own ghillie suit to dress up for the costume contest at the Bigfoot festival each year instead of using one of those cheesy onesie outfits that anyone can buy off Amazon. They're a dead-ringer for the real deal.

Dad quickly calculates Mr. Atkins's total, and before I know it, my favorite teacher is exiting through the front door. The rest of the evening goes by without incident—unless you count Riley selecting a spot in the center of the shop to urinate. Poor girl has trouble holding it in these days. Once the analog clock above the cash register strikes eight, it's closing time, and I follow Dad and Riley out the front door onto the wraparound porch.

I file into Mom's Beetle while Dad locks up with Riley at his side, and I watch from the driver's seat as they both get inside Dad's pickup. He doesn't take off right away, staying behind to make sure my car starts up without issue so I'm not left stranded in the parking lot. On the second try, the engine hums to life, and I'm following behind my dad's dusty old Tacoma as we head back home. Soon enough, we'll be munching on a microwave meal in front of the blue glow of our tiny television screen before marching off to bed, ready to do it all over again the next day.

As I slip beneath the covers and prepare to drift off to sleep, all the things I've tried not to think about creep out from the corners of my mind. I ping-pong between flashes of Asher Pope and his dead sister, Carissa and Kate, Simon and that poor girl in Saranac Lake, tossing and turning to shake each image away. Finally, my body stills and breath slows as my thoughts settle on my interaction with Mr. Atkins at the shop—the only positive thing to happen all day. My heart flutters when I recall the way he winked at me. How his fingers grazed mine. What he said to me after I thanked him for his help.

"Call me Dave."

Maybe it's wrong to think about my math teacher this way, but I don't care. He's the only thing keeping the monsters away from my mind right now. Besides, no one else has to know that his face is the last thing I think about before surrendering to slumber.

I've got plenty of secrets, it seems—what's one more?

Chapter 5

I don't have the nightmare again, which means I don't spend the morning sulking in bed, so I have time to sit at the breakfast table and eat with Dad before heading out the door. Today's menu features a stack of fluffy flapjacks smothered in melted butter and homemade maple syrup from Aunt Josie who lives across the state line in Fair Haven. I remember running between the sap lines in her forest full of hearty maple trees when I was a kid as she showed me how to drill holes through the bark and insert the tubes to drain the trunks of their liquid treasure. From what I remember, it's a lot of hard work, which is why she's able to charge fifty dollars a gallon for it at her farm stand. But we get it for free, so I don't feel guilty when I let

Riley lick my plate clean after I've swallowed the last bite of pancake.

"I'm going to Simon's today after school," I remind Dad as I bring my plate to the sink and start scrubbing away the remnants of sticky syrup that Riley's tired tongue couldn't scrape away.

"Okay, but don't be too late," Dad warns. "I don't like the thought of you being out at night in that junker."

I roll my eyes and scoot out of the way as Dad joins me at the sink so he can wash his plate.

"You act like he lives *so* far away," I grumble. "Even if I had to walk, it's just a couple of blocks across town. Whitehall's, what? Five square miles of houses? Big whoop. I'll be fine."

"Just... humor me, okay? Be back before nine at least. I worry about you, you know? You're all I've got."

I watch his throat bobble as he swallows back the urge to shed a tear. The significance of his statement is enough to suck all the natural light from the room that spills in through the windows behind the breakfast nook in the corner. It's all I can do not to cry. I bury my head in his chest and wrap my arms around him.

"I'll be home before nine," I promise. We latch onto each other for a moment longer but break away before it's too late and we refuse to let go. I try not to look at him as

I head out to the foyer and lace up my sneakers. I'm afraid that if I do, I'll start sobbing and I won't be able to stop. Riley hobbles out to join me while I pop my feet into my shoes. She senses my melancholy and when I bend down to tie my laces, she plants a slobbery kiss on my cheek, instantly replacing my sadness with revulsion.

"Gross, Riley," I moan. "You eat your own poop, for crying out loud!"

She pants in my face, her hot breath punctuating my statement as the scent of what I'm sure is fecal matter mingles with the maple syrup she just lapped up and wafts up my nostrils. I'll never understand how an animal so cute can also be so disgusting. I do my best to tie my sneakers without vomiting now that a cloud of Riley's rotten breath is hovering around my head like a swarm of stinky mosquitoes. When I'm done, I head out the door, calling over my shoulder to say goodbye to Dad as I climb into the Beetle, which somehow starts up just fine this morning despite the chill in the air.

By the time I park the car and head inside the school, there's still a good twenty minutes to kill until first period starts. Instead of going straight to my locker, I navigate through the throng of students milling about the hallway until I arrive at Simon's locker. I catch him just as he's shoving the last of his textbooks into his backpack and slamming the metal door shut with a loud clang. As soon as he lays eyes on me, the corners of his mouth get pinned into his cheeks and I can't help but smile back.

"Hey, Si."

"Hey, yourself! You ready to do the show tonight?" He asks me this every week, and every week I say the same thing.

"You know it!" I try to sound as enthusiastic as I know I should be, but if I'm telling the truth, no part of me is interested in doing our paranormal podcast today. Even though the nightmare didn't make a repeat performance last night, I'm still shaken up about Simon's story from yesterday. How similar it was to what happened to Renée. How her brother is now my English teacher. How Simon still insists on making Asher Pope the guest for our live show at the festival. Normally, the podcast is something I look forward to each week, but right now, it's hitting a little too close to home for me. And Simon can sense it.

"What's wrong?" His dark brows pull together as he fixes me with a skeptical stare.

"Nothing," I lie. His eyebrows relax a bit, but I can still see the doubt in his eyes when he looks at me. He knows me too well, which is something I usually take comfort in, but right now, I just wish he'd stop staring at me like that.

Like he can see something is bothering me. Like he wants to know what it is, and I can't tell him.

I hate keeping secrets.

He finally shrugs away the concern and slings an arm around my shoulder, steering me back down the hallway from where I just came so we can head to my locker. As we walk, he chats excitedly about what he has planned for the show.

"I know we were gonna talk about the Abair Road incident to tease the festival and all, but I thought of something even better."

"Better than the most credible Bigfoot sighting in Whitehall history?" I cast a dubious glance in his direction, not bothering to disguise the incredulity and slight annoyance that his sudden change of plans has spurred in me. Even though I wasn't particularly excited about today's show, I still have the notes I prepared tucked away inside my backpack. Now he's telling me all that work I did—all the hours spent reading the various accounts online; hunting down Mr. Gosselin's phone number so I could talk to him about what he and the other police officers on duty saw during that fateful summer in 1976—all of that had been for nothing. What the heck?

"I know, I know, but hear me out." Simon leans in a bit closer and lowers his voice. "What if we do a show all about what happened to Renée Pope instead? Get people *really* excited for what we've got planned for the festival?"

I stop dead in my tracks, which forces Simon's arm to fall from around my shoulder as he keeps moving forward. He spins around to face me, confusion written all over his features as he blinks in my direction.

"I don't know about that, Si." I bite my lip. "I think it's still too fresh for everyone. We agreed when we started this that we wouldn't—"

"Well, that was before." Simon folds his arms across his chest in defiance.

"Before what?"

"Before Asher Pope showed up to hand us a guaranteed hit show on a silver platter," he deadpans.

"Simon..."

"Look, I know you're all nervous to talk to him and whatever, but this is too good of an opportunity, E. We have to take it."

"I'm *not* nervous to talk to him," I lie to him for a second time this morning. "I'm just... I did so much work on the Abair story already. I got some great sound bites from my conversation with Mr. Gosselin. It's a great story. Can't we just stick to the original plan? I mean, the Abair case is the whole reason the festival exists in the first place. We've gotta cover it."

Simon takes a step toward me and places his arm back around my shoulder, using his free hand to push his thick, black glasses up the bridge of his beak.

"You're right," he admits to my utter amazement.

"Really?"

"Yeah, totally." He grins, and I already know what he's going to say next before the words leave his lips. "But we're still doing the Renée story this week instead. We have to, E. You know I'm right. We can do the Abair story next week, okay? Promise."

I throw my head back, pinching Simon's scrawny arm between my neck as I do so, and let out a low groan.

"Fine," I grumble. "But if we're doing this, we need to be smart about it, okay? Like maybe we change the names and locations or something so the locals don't get offended. I don't want to get on anyone's bad side over this."

Simon can't hold back the snort that escapes from his hawkish nose.

"What? Like you're on anyone's *good* side these days?" he teases.

"Shut up," I push his arm off my shoulder as we arrive at my locker and he laughs at the curt expression on my face.

"Oh, c'mon," he whines. "You know I'm only joking."

"Ha, ha." I roll my eyes at him before entering my locker combination. I'm still giving Simon the side eye as my locker door swings open, so I don't see what's sitting inside it at first. But once I do, the whole world comes to a stop. A flood of dread washes over me from my scalp to my toes, like I've walked into a booby trap and a bucket full of ice-cold water has just been dropped over my head. I feel my stomach flip as the color evaporates from my cheeks.

This can't be happening.

But it is happening. Staring down at me from the top shelf of my locker is a can of Fix-A-Flat, which would be weird enough on its own, but that's not what makes my heart stop beating. It's what's taped around the canister that freezes the flow of blood through my veins. Wrapped around the metal cylinder is a black-and-white photo of Renée Pope printed on a piece of copy paper. Beneath it is a handwritten message that makes me want to scream when I read it:

I KNOW WHAT YOU DID.

"What're you looking at?" Simon's voice sends a jolt of panic down my spine and I slam my locker shut before he can see what's inside. I can't let him see it. Can't let him see the tears that are starting to burn at the back of my eyes.

"I left something in my car," I mutter before bolting down the hallway, leaving Simon standing speechless by my locker as I weave through the crowd of students with reckless abandon. I don't even feel it when Brittany Wheeler knocks into me with her shoulder on my way out the double glass doors. I hold it together for as long as I can, but by the time I fling the car door open and drop into the driver's seat of Mom's old Beetle, I can hardly see through the tears spilling down my cheeks. There are less than five minutes left until first period, and I know Mrs. Morton won't be as forgiving of my tardiness this time, but I don't care. I can't go back inside that building. Not when there's someone inside who knows what I've tried so hard to keep hidden. But that's the thing about small towns.

Nothing stays hidden forever.

Chapter 6

Eventually, I calm down enough to go to class, and Mrs. Morton isn't happy when I walk in late to her lecture. Whatever. It's not like I would have learned anything if I had shown up on time. All I can think about is that note in my locker and who might have sent it. The words echo around in my skull like a gunshot ricocheting off the craggy surface of a nearby mountain.

I know what you did.

I try to tell myself that it's just a sick prank. Someone trying to mess with me. Scare me. If that is the case, then I guess I should congratulate them because it's working. I'm terrified. But I know that this isn't a practical joke. This isn't a coincidence. This is real—the Fix-A-Flat proves it.

But how? More importantly, *who?*

In all the years that have passed since it happened, I never said a word to anyone. And believe me, I wanted to. It's not easy to carry guilt like this around all the time. It eats at you, jerks you awake at night, makes your skin feel like it's going to crawl right off your bones. There have been so many times when I almost spilled the beans to Simon, but I couldn't. Not just because I was afraid of what he might think, but because I promised that I wouldn't speak a word of it to anyone—ever.

We all did.

That's when it hits me: There are only two other people in the entire world who know about what happened. Two people who love to torment me almost as much as they enjoy their continued status as the most popular girls in school. Two people who I royally pissed off yesterday in math class when I dared to stand up for myself. Maybe this *is* a prank, after all. Maybe I went too far, and they're trying to teach me a lesson. Put me back in my place. Remind me of the dirt they have on me.

I'm so convinced that this is what happened that I consider skipping pre-calculus altogether just so I can avoid another run-in with Carissa and Kate. Maybe I'll feign an illness and convince Mr. Atkins to send me to the nurse's office. Then I won't have to risk getting in trouble on top of everything else. No one's going to punish a sick kid. It's decided. As soon as I walk into Mr. Atkins's classroom, I'll march right up to his desk—no, not march. Sick kids don't march. I'll limp or hobble or something. Yeah, that's it. I'll hobble over to his desk with my arms clenched around my stomach and I'll—

SLAM!

I don't even make it all the way to Mr. Atkins's classroom before I feel two pairs of hands shove me into the nearest locker. All the bones in my body turn to liquid when I realize that it's Carissa and Kate.

Crap.

"Do you think you're funny?" Carissa sneers. I swallow around the bile that I can feel climbing higher up my esophagus.

"Um, I... uh..."

"*Um, um, um,*" Carissa mocks me before tapping me on the side of the skull with the open palm of her perfectly manicured hand. "Spit it out, idiot!"

"I–I don't know w–what you're talking about," I stammer, straightening my back as I try to push through them and get to the safety of Mr. Atkins's classroom.

"Bull!" Kate pins me back against the locker, keeping a firm grip on my shoulder as her eyes narrow on me. "We know that you're the one who—"

"Shut up, Kate," Carissa snaps. "Let me handle this."

Kate's jaw tightens as she clamps down on whatever words she wants to say but thinks better of it. A flash of Kate's younger self darts through my mind, and I wonder if Carissa sees it, too. Whitehall isn't the type of place that most people think of when they hear "New York." It's Podunk. Hillbilly, some might say. *The Smallest Town in New York.* All those bright lights and speeding taxies and towering skyscrapers—all that stuff is just a tiny part of a much vaster landscape. But it's the part that Kate knows best because it's the part she used to call home before she moved here after her twelfth birthday.

I remember when she first arrived in town. She had this attitude about her, this *confidence* that I didn't think was possible for someone her age to possess. Like she carried a piece of the city with her wherever she went. Maybe that's why I gravitated toward her so much. She was everything I wanted to be—pretty and self-assured and cultured. But most of all, she was feisty. She didn't take anyone's crap back then, least of all Carissa's. It didn't take her long to learn her place, though. It's no coincidence that Carissa's last name is King. Her family might as well be royalty as far as this town is concerned.

"Let's go, ladies!" Mr. Atkins's voice calls to us down the hallway. "I don't want to have to write you up. Get a move on. It's time for class."

Once again, I'm grateful for his intervention, but the relief doesn't have a chance to fully bloom inside my chest before Carissa's eyes are back on me, turning my blood cold in an instant.

"We aren't finished," she growls. "Since you're feeling so *nostalgic* today, why don't you meet us at the trailhead to Death Rock after school?"

I don't know what Carissa means by "nostalgic," but the sound of her selected meeting spot sends shivers down my spine, and not just because of its ominous name.

"I can't today," I sputter. "I have to—"

"I don't give a crap about whatever little plans you *think* you had," she spits. "Death Rock. Three o'clock. Don't be late, or we'll come find you."

She gives me one last shove into the locker before linking arms with Kate and marching off to class. My legs are rubber when I summon the courage to peel myself off the wall and file into the classroom behind them.

I don't have a clue what Mr. Atkins taught in class today. Pre-calculus is the furthest thing from my mind as I glide through the hallway like a ghost after class lets out and

I inevitably deposit myself into the empty seat next to Simon's in Mrs. Sneider's classroom.

"You don't look so good." His nose crinkles as the comment leaves his lips.

"I don't *feel* so good," I murmur. He scrunches his eyebrows together and leans forward so his body spills over the edge of his desk and hovers over mine.

"Is everything okay? You ran away from me this morning like I had the plague or something. If this is about the show, we can do the Abair case instead if you're really that upset about it. I don't mind. I just thought that—"

"It's not about the show," I say a little too harshly and instantly regret it, sinking my head into my hands. "I'm sorry," I groan. "It's just... something happened."

Simon's fingers lace around my wrist as he gently pries my hands away from my face.

"What happened? You know you can tell me anything." The way he says it, I almost believe him. I want to get it all off my chest right then and there, but I can't. Especially not after I see Mr. Pope watching us from the doorway to the classroom. I decide to tell Simon a half-truth instead.

"Carissa and Kate have it out for me," I tell him. He rolls his eyes and leans back into his chair.

"Tell me something I *don't* already know," he says.

"This is different," I argue. "They're pissed at me. Like *really pissed*. They want me to meet them at Death Rock after school, and they said if I don't go, they're gonna like... hunt me down or something, I don't know."

Simon gives me an uneasy look and bites down on his bottom lip.

"I don't like the sound of that," he comments. Now it's my turn to roll my eyes.

"And you think *I* do?" I cover my head in my hands again. "I don't know what I'm gonna do."

"Maybe we should tell someone," Simon suggests. "Like a teacher or something. I don't know. This sounds like it could be bad."

"Oh yeah, *there's* a great idea," I say sarcastically. "You know that's just gonna make them even angrier. There's no avoiding it. I have to do this. If I don't, I'm as good as dead anyway."

Simon goes quiet. He knows I'm right. When Carissa and Kate tell you to do something, you do it, or you pay the consequences. Another moment of silence passes and I peek through my fingers to see if my friend is even still sitting next to me. When I spy him through the slits in my fingers, I see him rifling through my backpack.

"What're you doing?"

"Looking for your phone," he answers.

"It's right here," I say, reaching into my back pocket before passing the device to him discretely so Mr. Pope can't see. Simon snatches it out of my hand and tries to open it but is stymied by the need for a password. He waves the locked screen at me as if to say, *What's your code?* And I tell him 091618. September 16, 2018. The day Mom died.

Once he's in, Simon taps away at my screen and hands the phone back to me just before the bell rings and Mr. Pope closes the door on whatever poor stragglers didn't make it to class in time.

"What was that about?" I whisper.

"I turned on Share My Location to track you," Simon mutters. "This way I'll know if anything goes wrong."

I slip the phone back inside my back pocket and spend the entire class trying to convince myself that Simon's just being overly cautious. But somehow I know that he's not being paranoid. I'm in danger.

And there's nothing I can do about it.

Chapter 7

The dirt road that leads to Death Rock is long and winding, with towering pines that loom overhead and block out the sun. Pebbles kick up in the wheel beds of Mom's old Beetle as I inch along the dusty path that spans parallel to the Champlain Canal and inevitably branches off to South Bay. The entire time I drive, I pray for a sudden breakdown to keep me from reaching my final destination. Sasquatch are thought to be nocturnal creatures, with most sightings occurring well after the sun has dipped below the horizon. But even if they were known to come out during the day, I'd still prefer to risk an encounter with one of those hairy beasts than face the wrath of Carissa and Kate.

Unfortunately for me, Mom's car survives the trip without issue, placing me at the Death Rock trailhead a whole five minutes early—plenty of time for me to have a full-blown panic attack in the driver's seat. I try to focus on the way the choppy waters in South Bay lap at the rocky shoreline by the edge of the parking area rather than my impending doom, but its calming effect fails to ease the tension mounting in my chest. My heart is hammering so hard and so fast, it hurts to breathe, even as I cycle through the breathing exercises that my therapist taught me. Back when I still went to therapy.

I remember the first time I had a panic attack. It was the day of Mom's funeral. The funeral parlor was dim and dreary, contained in a narrow Victorian manor right off Main Street in the heart of the village. Dad and I sat in the front row at the viewing, surrounded by floral wallpaper and softly glowing chandeliers that seemed too sad to illuminate the space. Like the crystal beads were teardrops trapping the light that tried to escape from each bulb. Mom lay inside a mahogany box at the front of the room, her coffin decorated with sunflowers and white lilies. When it was time for me and Dad to go pay our respects, that's when it happened. The muscles around my sternum pinched and squeezed at my heart. Palpitations fluttered through my chest with every step I took toward the casket. By the time we reached her side, the pain in my heart was so sharp, the nausea so intense, and my vision so dizzy, I thought for sure that I was having a heart attack. I waited until she was buried to say anything about it. I didn't want to take the attention off of Mom. Dad was furious with me for keeping it secret.

"What if you were having heart failure?" he had hollered at me. It was one of the only times that he'd ever raised his voice to me. I knew it was just because he was scared. He had already lost the love of his life; he couldn't stomach the thought of losing his twelve-year-old daughter on top of it.

The doctors in the emergency room placed these weird stickers all over my chest with tiny metal buttons in the middle, which they hooked up to a bunch of scary-looking wires. They called it an EKG—"standard procedure," they assured me—but it didn't feel standard. It just made me even more nervous. When the results came in, they informed me that it hadn't been a heart attack at all. It was "just a panic attack." *Just.* Like they're easy to live through. Like they don't take your breath away each time they come, even after you learn how to breathe in through your nose and out through your mouth, counting the seconds until it passes. Like I was being dramatic for wasting their time on something so trivial. So "treatable" as they had called it.

I started therapy the following week, and that's where I learned about the breathing exercises. My doctor wanted to put me on medication, but I didn't want anything to do with it. I was pretty popular back then, and I didn't want the kids at school to judge me for being so crazy that I needed to take pills to calm myself down. So, I learned to deal with it in my own way instead. I only went to a few sessions. Something about unloading all my problems onto a total stranger never felt quite right to me. Maybe that's just my small-town mentality—in a rural community like ours, people learn to solve their own problems, and they rarely ask for help doing it. But every now and then when I feel an attack coming on, I go back to that therapist's office and remember the way her gentle voice guided me through each breath, helping me regain my composure.

I'm gulping down a fresh intake of air through my nose when I hear the crunch of tires rolling across the gravel lot where I'm parked. As I release the breath out through my mouth, I resist the urge to start the car back up and peel away before Carissa and Kate can drag me out of the driver's seat.

Let's get this over with.

"You've got a lot of nerve, Little Miss Liza Lot," Carissa barks as the car door slams behind me. She marches around the front of her shiny, silver Mercedes Coupe to join Kate by the passenger side door. They fold their arms in identical fashion, a united front of hatred pointed in my direction.

"What the hell do you think you're doing pulling a stunt like that anyway?"

I swallow hard, trying to dissolve the tremor in my throat that I know will be there when I speak, but my voice still comes out shaky and weak when I form the words.

"Look, I'm sorry about yesterday, okay? I didn't mean to stare at you and Joel, and I'm sorry for telling you to shut up. Can we drop it now?"

Carissa's eyes narrow like she's looking at either the ugliest thing she's ever seen or the stupidest. Either way, it doesn't feel great to be on the receiving end of her icy stare.

"That's not what I'm talking about, *moron*," she growls. "I know it's hard for you, but please. Don't play dumb."

My cheeks flush pink at the insult, and my rising anger gives me the courage to stand a little taller. I cross my arms over my chest, mirroring their posture as I dig my heels into the gravel and level Carissa with my best attempt at an intimidating stare.

"I don't know what you're talking about," I tell her.

"Liar!" Kate spits. She leans in closer and I have to clench to keep from urinating. The way she looks at me with that inner-city scowl etched into her face makes me feel like I might be headed straight to the bottom of South Bay. I shrink away, stopping only when the hard surface of Mom's Beetle presses against my back.

"I swear to God, I'm not lying," I insist, but Carissa and Kate don't want to hear it. They creep closer to me, shadows from the tree branches overhead making their angry faces look even more menacing.

"Okay, fine," Carissa coos, the slight edge in her soft voice telling me that it's not "fine" at all. "But if you're not lying, then that means you told someone. And you know what that means?"

An evil smile stretches across Carissa's glossy lips and somehow snakes its way over to Kate's face.

Oh God. They're going to kill me.

"It means you're *dead*," Kate confirms the panicked thoughts racing through my mind and my heart skips several beats.

"Please," I beg. "I really don't know what you're—"

I stop before I can complete the statement because that's when I realize that I *do* know what they're talking about. Suddenly, all of Carissa's words begin to make a lot more sense as they replay through my mind one after the other.

Since you're feeling so nostalgic *today... Pulling a stunt like that... You told someone... You know what that means?*

"Enough of this," Carissa announces. "If she's not gonna admit to it, we'll just have to teach her a lesson. Kate, grab her. Let's see how loud this little *freak* can scream."

"Wait!" I yelp as Kate reaches out to wrap her hands around me. "Did you guys get a... did you find a note in your locker this morning?"

"Oh, *now* you remember," Kate leers at me.

"What was the plan anyway?" Carissa throws her hands up to the sky. "Did you think you could just threaten us and *poof!* Back to the top of the food chain for Liza Lot? That's not how this works. You made a pact that day. We all did. You broke it, and now you have to pay."

Kate lunges forward and I scamper away before she can grab me. She lands with a thud against the driver's side door of Mom's car as I back away with slow, deliberate steps, placing as much distance as I can between me and the two wolves in my midst while still trying to reason with them.

"Please, *please* just listen to me," I implore. "I've never told *anyone* about that night. I swear on my mom's grave, I've never told a soul. Why would I risk that? I'd get in just as much trouble as you guys if anyone ever found out."

"So why put the notes in our locker then?" Kate challenges.

"I didn't put the notes in your locker!" I protest.

"Then how did you know we even got them?" Carissa bites back. "See, Kate? She's lying. Let's just finish this already. I'm bored."

"No! Listen to me!" I try to tell them that they have it all wrong. I got a note, too. I'm just as much a victim as they are. But they don't want to hear it. They already have their minds made up. And if I don't get out of here fast, I'm a goner.

In the blink of an eye, Kate races forward with all the determination of a hungry lioness ready to take down the helpless gazelle in her sights. I'm a good fifteen feet ahead of her, which gives me a decent head start as I race away in the opposite direction back toward the dirt road that delivered me to this literal hell on earth. My car keys dig into my thigh with each pump of my legs as I run as fast as I can through the gnarled pines flanking either side of the road. There's no time to negotiate a route back to the safety of Mom's car. I need to keep moving. I need to keep running. So I do. And I don't look back. Not even when I hear Carissa calling out to me in the distance.

"Run, run, as fast as you can!" she yells through the forest. "But you can't hide from us, Liza! We'll find you!"

I don't stop running until I emerge from the trees at the edge of Ridgeback Farms. The run from the Death Rock trailhead parking lot took at least twenty minutes, and even though it's a six-minute drive from the farm to Simon's house on Pauline Street, I don't have my car, so I don't reach the steps of his rickety front porch until it's five o'clock. My legs are so tired, the five steps that comprise the wooden staircase might as well be a mountain. Part of me thinks I might be better off going straight home, but I'm so shaken up right now, the thought of being alone scares me. I need to talk to someone. I need a friend.

I need to confess.

"E, what the heck happened to you?" Simon rips the front door nearly off its hinges as he ushers me into his house, his brown eyes filled with worry as he takes me in. "You look awful."

I know it's the truth. My skin is sticky with sweat from all the running and walking. My hair is windswept and tangled, and I wouldn't be surprised if there were a few pine needles trapped inside my tresses. And even though I know his observation is coming from a place of concern rather than judgment, I can't help the flood of tears that rises to the surface when he makes the comment. Before I can stop it from happening, saltwater is streaming down my cheeks and I'm gasping for air that doesn't seem like it will ever reach my lungs.

Simon's eyes go wide as he watches the breakdown unfold. He wraps his arms around me and hugs me tight to his chest, stroking my hair as I sob uncontrollably into his Iron Maiden tee shirt. As we stand in the foyer, I hear the distinct sound of running water and clattering dishes filtering into the room from the kitchen down the cramped, wood-paneled hallway.

"Simon, honey, is everything alright?" Mrs. Little calls out as she shuts the tap to listen for her son's reply. I feel his tiny muscles tighten around me at the sound of her voice and I do my best to stifle my sobs so she doesn't get suspicious. Simon's mom is a wonderful woman, but the last thing I need right now is to have an adult asking me a million questions about why I'm crying.

"Yeah, Mom, everything's fine," Simon lies. "It's just E. We're gonna go to the garage now to do the show."

There's a pause, and I imagine Mrs. Little standing at the kitchen sink, tilting her head full of spiky, black hair as though trying to decide whether or not her son is lying.

Finally, I hear the squeak of the knobs as she brings the faucet back to life so she can finish doing the dishes.

"Okay, honey, you two have fun," she says. Simon releases me from his embrace and grips me by the shoulders, spinning me around so we can file out through the front door. We don't say a word to one another as we step down from the porch and make our way to the detached garage that's tucked away at the end of the driveway to the left of the house. But as soon as we pile in through the side door and march up the unfinished wooden staircase to the enclosed loft that lives above the two-car garage, I'm back to crying.

Simon guides me to the beanbag sofa against the far side of the room, lowering me with care until the full weight of my body sinks into the squishy material. I cover my face with my hands and allow the tears to blind me. The sofa collapses a little lower as Simon takes a seat next to me and I feel his thin arm snake around my shoulders as he brings me close, his thumb tracing circles into my upper arm as he tries to calm me.

"E." His voice is soft when he speaks, like he's addressing a frightened toddler instead of a teenage girl. "You're scaring me. What happened out there? What did they do to you?"

My stomach somersaults with the memory of Carissa and Kate lunging after me, their accusations still so fresh in my mind, it's like I never left the Death Rock trailhead at all. A fresh deluge of tears quakes through my body as I think about what tomorrow might bring. Maybe I should have let them kill me in the woods. It's all I deserve anyway.

"Please say something," Simon begs. I press my fingertips deeper into my skull.

"I c–can't," I sputter. "I c–can't s–s–say it."

"Hey." Simon's hands find mine and he gently takes them away from my face, brushing the tears from my cheeks with the back of his hand. "I'm here for you, E. You can tell me anything."

Maybe it's my emotions running high or maybe it's the look of genuine concern, of caring, in Simon's eyes when he says the words. Whatever it is, a fire sparks somewhere deep inside my gut, and I believe him. So, I suck in a deep breath, press my head back into the sofa, and I do it.

I tell him everything.

Chapter 8

We were thirteen the night Renée Pope was attacked in the woods. It hadn't even been a full year since Mom died, and I was still feeling angry and hurt and lost. Instead of talking about it with anyone, I started to act out. Looking back on it now, I know it was stupid. But I was just so mad at everything. I guess I just felt like if the world could take away someone as kind and caring and beautiful as my mom, then what was the point of trying to be good? So, I decided to be bad.

And I liked it. I liked it a lot.

It started with dumb things. Choosing not to do my homework. Mocking some of the less popular girls in class for no reason while Carissa and Kate egged me on. Yup, that's right. Despite her daddy's status as the mayor of

Whitehall and landlord of half the properties in town, I was the leader of our little clique—not Carissa. Kind of hard to believe, I know. But that's the way it was. Before Mom died, being popular hadn't been synonymous with being vindictive and cruel. In fact, I tried hard to be as inclusive as possible, never leaving people out even if they weren't considered "cool." Carissa always hated that. She was more than eager to ostracize whomever she deemed to be unworthy of our friendship. As soon as I let my grief take over and began taking my aggression out on everyone else, Carissa was happy to go along for the ride, and Kate never raised any concerns about it. I guess she just missed the excitement of the city, and picking on country bumpkins was a good way to get a cheap thrill.

But pretty soon, the pettiness got old, and I needed something else to fill the void that Mom left behind. It wasn't long before I started creeping around the kitchen at night, poking around the liquor cabinet that Dad never bothered to lock until I found something bitter to choke down that could numb the pain I was feeling. I'd wait until he was fast asleep in his bedroom, sneak downstairs to the place where the whiskey was held, and stuff the bottle in my backpack before slipping out the side door in the kitchen into the velvet night. Swinging my legs over my blue bicycle, I'd pedal through the darkness with my bag full of liquor bouncing against my back, racing to meet up with Carissa and Kate so we could take turns seeing who could take the longest swig from the bottle without wincing.

We didn't want to risk getting seen by one of our parents' friends, so instead of meeting up at the marina or outside the Skenesborough Museum, we took cover in the woods. Sometimes we'd bike out to the railroad at the edge of The Saddles State Forest, but more often than not, we'd meet at the Death Rock trailhead. That's where we found ourselves the night Renée Pope died.

I didn't know Renée that well. She was a senior in high school while we were just kids messing around in the forest, pretending to be much older with our mouths full of stolen whiskey. When I saw Renée's white Honda parked at the edge of South Bay as I joined Carissa and Kate at the trailhead that night, I didn't even recognize it as her car. I just viewed it as another game to play. Another thrill to seek in my mission to smother the sadness I didn't want to acknowledge was there.

"Let's play a game," I announced, swallowing down a fresh gulp of brown liquor with a grimace.

"Yay!" Carissa squealed. The stench of whiskey from her breath hovered like a cloud in the humid night air still thick with heat from the summer sun. "What game should we play?"

"Truth or dare," I decided before Kate could speak.

"Oooh, this should be interesting," Carissa giggled. "Okay… Kate, truth or dare?"

Kate reached for the bottle in my hands and took a swig before choosing.

"Truth."

"Ugh, lame." Carissa rolled her eyes and snatched the bottle from Kate's hands. As she swished the whiskey around in her mouth, she contemplated the perfect question to ask. "Who do you have a crush on at school?"

Even with her brown skin hidden beneath the shadows of the forest, I could see Kate blush. She dipped her head into her hands, her palms muffling the sound of her mortified response.

"Tyler Jenkins," she admitted. Carissa and I burst out laughing and took another sip from the whiskey bottle, which Kate ripped out of my hands before I could finish swallowing.

"My turn now," she taunted. Her eyes lingered on Carissa for a moment and I could see the gears grinding away in her head as she pondered the likelihood that torturing the mean-spirited blonde would be worth the inevitable fallout. The last time Kate had given Carissa a taste of her own medicine, things didn't end so well.

Kate had pushed Carissa into a locker and screamed in her face after Carissa dared to make fun of the way Kate's mom spoke with a thick Jamaican accent. Growing up in a small town, I never learned the art of swearing. But that day, I learned a thing or two from Kate as she hurled profanities at Carissa while the petite blonde cowered in fear against the cold surface of the lockers that Kate had her pinned against. Sure enough, Carissa went crying to her daddy. One call to the principal's office was all it took for Kate to get suspended. She never went after Carissa again.

The memory of Carissa's victory must have been too fresh in Kate's mind because instead of selecting the wicked blonde as her target, she turned the spotlight on me.

"E—truth or dare?"

"Dare."

"Okay… I dare you to drink from this whiskey bottle for ten whole seconds." Kate shoved the bottle back into my hands, the glint of mischief in her eyes telling me that she expected me to protest. I didn't give her the satisfaction of trying to negotiate my way out of it. I brought the bottle to my lips and chugged while she and Carissa counted down each excruciating second in unison.

"Ten Mississippi, nine Mississippi, eight Mississippi…"

The alcohol burned all the way down my esophagus, landing with an unexpected heaviness in my gut. When the counting was finally over, I spat whatever whiskey was left in my mouth out to the ground, which Kate and Carissa thought was hilarious. I hunched over and gripped my knees, fighting the urge to vomit as I coughed around the bitterness. Miraculously, I didn't puke. On the contrary, I felt incredible as I straightened myself. Like I was invincible. Like I could do anything I wanted and not have to face any consequences.

And that's exactly what I did.

"Carissa—truth or dare." I eyed my friend through the moonlight and awaited her response, which didn't disappoint.

"Dare." Without hesitation, I issued the challenge.

"I dare you to slash that car's tires."

"*What?*" Carissa screeched. "No way!"

"You have to," I argued. "Those are the rules."

"Yeah." Kate joined me at my side. "Those are the rules."

Carissa's eyes darted nervously between me and Kate, waiting for one of us to back down, but we held firm in our resolve. "You guys suck," she whined. "I don't want to do this. What would I even do it with?"

"With my dad's hunting knife," I offered.

"So, you're gonna bike all the way home and all the way back, just to grab your dad's hunting knife for some stupid prank?"

"No, *moron*." I pushed past her to the backpack that was resting on the ground beside my bicycle. "I've got it right here. I always bring it with me when we go out at night. Just in case."

"Just in case you want me to commit a crime, you mean," Carissa grumbled.

"Don't be such a baby," I shot back over my shoulder. I grabbed the knife out of the front zipper on my backpack and flipped it open before handing it over handle side first so I didn't prick her fingers. She stood there for a moment in a state of stunned disbelief, staring down at the knife in her hand like it was going to leap out of her palm and stab her through the heart.

"I don't know about this," Carissa moaned.

"Fine," I snapped. "You don't wanna do it? Kate and I will tell the whole school that *you're* the one with a crush on Tyler Jenkins. Isn't that right, Kate?"

Carissa's eyes became two blue saucers, her mouth hanging open like a freshwater bass pulled from the depths of South Bay.

"Oh yeah, I'll vouch for that," Kate snickered.

"The choice is yours," I teased. "Slash the tires, or the whole school will think you're in love with the kid who still thinks farts are funny... no offense, Kate."

Carissa stomped her foot on the ground like a toddler on the verge of erupting in an unforgettable tantrum. Tossing her head back, she released a guttural grunt of frustration before spinning on her heel and marching off in the direction of the white sedan situated by the edge of the water. Kate and I trailed her from behind so we could watch the destruction.

Moonlight rippled across the water's glassy surface as Carissa inched closer to the car, the black outline of her dainty silhouette all Kate and I could see from our place beneath the trees. We watched as she crouched beside the driver's side tire and plunged the knife into the rubber with a groan. She remained on the ground, appearing to wrestle with the tire for a few moments.

"What's taking so long?" I yelled.

"I can't!" Carissa let out another aggravated growl "Ugh! It's stuck. I can't get it out. I need help."

Kate and I turned to one another and shrugged before walking over to the car. Sure enough, the knife was wedged deep inside the tire so that the hilt was pressed tight against the rubber. Together, Carissa, Kate, and I wrapped our hands around the handle and leaned back with all our might until the knife finally came free. A slow, steady hiss escaped through the puncture that Carissa had made as the air evaporated from the tire.

"There," she said when the noise stopped. "I did it. Happy now?"

"No." I shook my head. "You've still got three left."

"You can't be serious." Carissa's eyebrows shot up to her scalp.

"Do I look like I'm joking?"

"E, that's not fair! You saw how hard it was for me to do just one. I did it. Let's just keep playing the game."

"A dare's a dare," I insisted. "Do it, or you and Tyler will be farting together for the rest of your lives."

"Gross! You're being so rude right now. I can't do it by myself. This isn't fair!"

"Fine," I conceded. "If it's really that hard, we'll do it together. That fair enough for you?"

"Wait, what?" Kate stammered.

"I said we'll do it together," I repeated. "You have a problem with that?"

"N–no, I—"

"Great, then it's settled. We'll do the rest as a team."

And so it went. I grabbed the knife from Carissa's hand and sank the tip of the blade into the back left tire. Together, we wrestled the knife free and listened as the air drained from the rubber vessel. Next was Kate, who tore through the front tire on the passenger's side. Again, we pulled the blade out as a team and waited for the tire to deflate. For the last tire, we took the plunge together, ripping it out almost as quickly as we sank it in. Before long, all four tires were completely depleted of air. It was done.

Maybe it was the unsettling silence that filled the air after the last tire finished hissing out its final breath or maybe we just didn't want to stick around to find out if whoever owned the car would show up and discover what we had done. Whatever the reason, we didn't linger at the trailhead for too much longer after that.

Carissa and Kate mounted their bikes and took off down the dirt road to make the twenty-minute trip back to town through the pitch-black forest. I tried to do the same, but all the chugging from the liquor bottle during our game of Truth or Dare had caught up to me by that point. My vision was so blurry, my equilibrium so off-balance, the moment I attempted to pedal away from the scene, I tipped over and skinned my knee badly. I couldn't see through the darkness, but I could tell from the slow, steady drip that ran down my shin that I was bleeding. Kate and Carissa were long gone by that point, so I had no choice but to limp my way home.

In the dark.

Completely alone.

When most people think of the woods, they probably imagine a small grouping of trees planted with care at the edge of a quiet suburb. A nice place to take a walk through a cemented trail where the only dangerous creatures are the mosquitoes that leave painful bites along your skin that itch for days on end. But out here, the woods mean something else entirely—especially at night.

It's dark. So dark, it sometimes feels like your eyes are closed, even though you can feel yourself blinking. So dark that when you tilt your head up to the sky, you can't even see the stars shining back at you through the branches overhead. And it's loud. Most people might assume it's quiet, but they'd be wrong (unless it's winter, of course, and all the animals are in hibernation—or dead).

But it wasn't winter as I hobbled through the forest that night. It was early September, and the woods were still alive with the feeling of summer. Insects chirped out their screechy songs in a horrifying symphony that made my skin feel buggy. Every few steps, I'd hear the low, throaty hoot of an owl calling out from high up in the pine trees. Twigs snapped with a horrible echo that made my stomach turn to ice each time an animal made their presence known. But what terrified me the most weren't the sudden cracks of tree branches breaking or the ominous chorus of nocturnal birds and insects. It was the strange, almost oppressive knowledge that even though there were no other people around for miles, I wasn't alone.

Something was out there. I could feel it. Watching me.

I was midway through the long walk from the trailhead to the main road when I heard the scream. At first, I thought it was just a fox. That's what I tried to convince myself, at least. Foxes sound an awful lot like a shrieking woman when they're trying to mate. But the more I listened, the more apparent it became that it wasn't a fox at all. It was a person. There was no doubt about it.

My first thought was that it might have been Carissa or Kate. Maybe one of them had tried to bike through the forest, trying to cut a more direct path through the trees to get home quicker. I couldn't just leave my friend stranded in the woods. No one else knew we were out there. I had to do something, even if I was blind drunk and too useless to even bike home myself.

As the shrieking continued, I decided to step off the main road and into the forest, abandoning my bike and following the noise until I found its source. I don't know if I was just too intoxicated or on some level I knew that it was best to keep quiet, but I didn't call out to whoever it was that was screaming. And it's a good thing I didn't because when I finally reached the place where the shrieking was coming from, that's when I saw it.

Being out in the woods for so long had given my eyes time to adjust to the darkness, even if I was still a little drunk and delirious. Despite my inebriated state, I could make out a small clearing in the trees through the shadows. Slivers of moonlight spilled through the tall branches overhead, landing with a silvery glow on what looked to be a white blanket lying on the ground. I didn't understand what I was looking at, but as I inched forward, squinting through the blackness, my intestines started to twist in knots. Because it wasn't a blanket at all.

It was a body.

And standing over it was the hairy, horrifying silhouette of a bipedal beast the likes of which I had only ever seen standing outside of the Bigfoot Museum down the road from where I lived.

Its massive body loomed over the pale and broken limbs lying at its enormous feet, a sickening ripping noise emanating from its claws as it tore at its victim. As it worked, I could hear it grunting and growling in a feral frenzy, like it was Christmas morning and the body on the forest floor was a brightly wrapped present that it couldn't wait to tear into. I froze in place, rubbing my eyes in an effort to wipe away the illusion that I still wasn't convinced was real.

But no matter how many times I tried to rid myself of the horror standing before me, it wouldn't go away. Because it wasn't just a drunken fantasy. It was real. I was watching a sasquatch rip its victim to shreds right before my eyes.

And I was completely and utterly alone.

Before I could stop myself, I opened my mouth to unleash a blood-curdling scream of my own. What other reaction could I have to a literal monster in my midst? Wolf spiders the size of nickels crawling up my shower wall were enough to coax a deafening shriek from my throat, let alone a seven-foot-tall apelike animal feasting on human flesh in the forest. As my jaw unhinged and I drew in a breath to scream, I felt a pair of hands reach out from the shadows and wrap themselves around my mouth, stopping the noise before it could leave my body.

My blood ran cold, heartbeat skipped around like a stone bouncing over the smooth, glassy surface of South Bay. First I had found a bigfoot, now I was being kidnapped? This couldn't be happening. The hands remained clamped around my mouth as panicked breath pumped in and out through my nose. I could feel myself being drawn into a tiny torso as the owner of the hands around my face brought me closer to their chest.

"I'm going to let go now," a voice whispered so softly in my ear that at first, I thought that I'd imagined it. "But you can't scream. It'll hear you."

With that, the hands released me and I spun around to see Simon's terrified face staring back at me. I didn't know Simon that well at the time, aside from the fact that he was the kid who everyone at school agreed was too bizarre to be friends with. Always spouting off tall tales about ghosts and ghouls and whatever other spooky nonsense we all thought was too weird for words. I had never really paid him much attention before that night. I had never thought of him as anything other than the weird kid with creepy parents who fed into his lies with that stupid sasquatch museum of theirs. But as we stood hidden behind the pine trees and watched in horror as the impossible transpired just thirty feet from where we remained concealed, I started to wonder if there was more truth than I wanted to admit to his stories.

We waited for what felt like hours as the monster finished its feast. But even when it had thundered off through the woods, leaving the body behind in its wake, we remained frozen in fear, too scared to move in case it heard us and came barreling back through the trees to turn us into its next set of victims. Thirty minutes passed before we thought it was safe to move. Neither of us spoke as we crept through the forest back to the main road where my bike was still waiting for me, but Simon stayed by my side the entire way home. I snuck back into my sleeping house and crawled into bed, too numb and terrified to feel the burn of my skinned knee as I hugged my legs to my chest and cried myself to the point of exhaustion.

That was the first time I had my nightmare.

The next day, I felt horrible. My stomach was sour from all the drinking, and I felt like I was going to throw up all over the place. But even if I hadn't been hungover, the fear alone would have been enough to make me nauseous. I thought about asking Dad if I could take a sick day and stay home, but it was only the first week of the school year and I knew he wouldn't let me, so I just sucked it up and went. Even if I had stayed home, it wouldn't have made a difference.

I still would have found out that Renée Pope was killed.

"My dad said they found the body in the woods!"

"She went out for a hike and never came home."

"They found her car at the trailhead with its tires slashed."

"The police think it's all connected somehow."

Bits of gossip filled the hallways as my classmates swapped stories about what had happened to the poor girl whose body was found in the woods by the park ranger that morning. It didn't matter that we were all in middle school and Renée was five years our senior. In a small town like Whitehall, when one kid goes missing or turns up dead, every kid feels it. Every kid talks about it. And with every new spin on the same tale, one common theme remained: Renée's death was no accident.

She was murdered. And whoever slashed her tires was the person responsible.

When lunchtime finally arrived, I still couldn't stomach the thought of eating. All I could think about was what I had seen in the woods the night before. What I had done. And I wasn't the only one who felt haunted by the previous night's events. Even though they hadn't been with me to witness what had really happened to Renée, Carissa and Kate sat ashen and quiet in their seats across the table from me in the cafeteria that day. We didn't say anything to one another for almost the entire lunch period, too caught up in our individual thoughts to give our fear a name. Kate was the first to break the silence.

"Do you think… it's 'cause of what we did?" She didn't need to clarify the question. We all knew what she meant. It's all any of us could think about.

Carissa leaned in and spoke in a low, harsh whisper.

"We can't tell anybody about what happened last night. They'll think we had something to do with it."

Kate and I exchanged a nervous glance. We knew she was right, but something about keeping a secret that big still felt wrong.

"Maybe if we just explain—"

"Explain what, E?" Carissa hissed. "That we were out in the woods drinking your dad's whiskey and thought it might be fun to… do what we did? Like anyone would believe us."

She crossed her arms and sat back in her chair with a huff. I knew she was right. Even though our prank hadn't been targeted at Renée, it didn't matter. We were still responsible. Because if it hadn't been for us, she might have found her way back to a working car that night. She might have started it up and sped out of there without falling into that monster's clutches.

If it hadn't been for us, she might still be alive.

"You're right," I admitted. "We can't tell anyone. Ever. It needs to stay a secret."

"More than a secret," Carissa added. "It's a promise. A pact. No one says a word. And if they do?"

She brought an index finger to her neck and dragged it across her throat, the action having the precise effect she wanted as shivers rattled down my spine and I could see Kate's skin turn several shades paler than her usual caramel complexion. It was decided. We wouldn't speak a word of what we had done to anyone. And if any of us did, there would be hell to pay.

Lunch ended and the three of us were headed back to class when I overheard a commotion coming down the hallway. I turned my head to see what was going on, and my gaze landed on a group of students circling around a frail and frightened-looking Simon like a shiver of sharks as they pushed him up against the lockers.

"It's the truth!" I heard him whining. "I saw it!"

"Shut up, *freak!*" Dave Truman shoved Simon so hard that his glasses slid off his face and clattered at his feet to the floor. "You're nothing but a liar looking for attention."

"No, I'm not," Simon shot back. "I saw Bigfoot last night, and I'm not the only one who saw it."

"Oh yeah?" Dave mocked. "Who else was with you then?"

Simon squinted past Dave's shoulder, his vision no doubt blurred by the absence of his prescription lenses.

But even with his sight impaired, he was able to pick me out of the crowd of students now gathered around to watch the fight scene unfold. He raised his hand and pointed in my direction as if in slow motion.

"She was," Simon asserted. "Eliza was with me in the woods last night. She saw it, too."

A hush fell over the crowd as everyone turned their heads in unison and waited to hear my response. I kept my eyes on the floor, refusing to speak, willing a teacher to intervene and save me from speaking a word. But the only thing I heard was the sound of Dave's taunting voice as he zeroed in on me.

"That true, Eliza?" he demanded. "You see a Sasquatch in the woods last night?"

"I—"

"Please, Eliza." Simon's gaze found mine, his eyes shiny with unshed tears as the bullies swarmed around him. "Tell them. Tell them what we saw."

Maybe it was the guilt pinching in my gut over the role I shared in contributing to Renée's death or maybe it was the fact that deep down, I knew I owed Simon my life. After all, if it hadn't been for him, I might have screamed, and that beast might have turned its sights on me next, leaving me broken and bloody in the woods. Before I had time to overthink it, I felt my lips start moving to form the words.

"Yeah," I confirmed. "I saw it, too."

Gasps erupted from the lips of every student as the significance of my confession crashed into them. But soon the shock was replaced with fresh mockery as I heard a sharp cackle rip through the air.

"Oh em *gee*, Eliza, you are *such* a weirdo!" Carissa teased, and the crowd burst out in laughter. My cheeks flushed crimson as I turned on my heel to face her.

"Shut up, Carissa," I snapped. "You're just jealous because you left before you could see it, too."

"Left?" She arched a golden eyebrow at me, a flash of panic darting through her eyes. "I don't know what you're talking about. I was at home all night. Nowhere near whatever little freak show you and Simon were putting on in the woods."

"That's not true," I insisted. "You and Kate—"

"Don't drag *me* into this." Kate put up her hands. "I was at home, too."

My eyes shifted from Carissa to Kate and back again, unable to believe that they were willing to make a liar out of me in front of the entire school. But as I silently begged them to come to my defense, I realized that they couldn't. Because if they did, it would mean that they were out in the woods that night, too, and we had all just agreed never to speak a word of it to anyone. There was nothing I could do but shrink away and accept my fate as my classmates turned on me one by one. They pointed and laughed, pushed and sneered, chanted with twisted glee, "Eliza Loft lies a lot! Eliza Loft lies a lot!"

In an instant, everyone had labeled me a liar. Everyone had written me off as crazy.

Everyone—except for Simon.

Chapter 9

When I finish telling Simon my story, it's so quiet, part of me wonders if he's still in the room. But I know that he is because I can still feel the depression of his body sitting next to me in the bean bag chair. I lift my head to face him, and the moment my gaze finds his, I instantly regret it. The way he's looking at me makes me feel like I'm the most horrible person in the world. No, it's worse than that. He looks at me like I'm not even a person at all. Like I'm a monster no different from that thing we saw in the woods all those years ago. Finally, he speaks, and I don't know which is worse: seeing the disdain in his eyes or hearing the disgust in his voice when he talks to me.

"What the hell, Eliza?" He never calls me that. It's always E. Ever since that day in school when I was dethroned and left to the wolves, he has always called me by my preferred nickname. Always stood by my side. But now? He hates me. And I can't even blame him for it, because I hate me, too.

"I know… it's so messed up." I sink my teeth into my bottom lip to keep the tears from spilling down my cheeks again. "But you have to believe me, Si. I didn't know it was her car. I didn't—"

"That's not the point," he snaps. I've never heard him sound so angry. So repulsed. It makes me want to curl up and die. "You would have done it to anyone. If it wasn't Renée, it would have been someone else that you…"

He doesn't finish the statement, and he doesn't have to. We both know what he was going to say. If it wasn't Renée, it would have been someone else that I trapped inside those woods. Someone else's life that I inadvertently ended with my actions. The thought makes me sick with anger. Anger at myself for being such a thoughtless, reckless idiot. Anger that I brazenly redirect at Simon because I'm so ashamed and I just want someone else to feel as horrible as I do.

"What about you, huh?" I huff. He scoffs at me as one of his dark brows shoots up to his hairline.

"What about me?"

"You were in the woods that night, too," I remind him. "What were you even doing out there anyway? How do I know *you* didn't do anything to keep Renée from getting out safely?"

His face crumples and I wish I could stuff the words back into my mouth. Why did I say that? No part of me believes that Simon could have done anything to cause Renée's death, even if it was something accidental. He's a good person. And I'm... I'm not.

"Simon, I'm sorry," I backtrack. "That was stupid. I didn't mean it. I—"

"Don't." He stops me before I can finish and the hurt in his eyes makes me want to cry. "You said it because you meant it. But unlike you, I don't have anything to hide about that night. Yeah, I was out there. I used to sneak out all the time and go roaming around the woods. It was the only way I thought that I could get the other kids at school to stop laughing at me. I thought if I could find something concrete, some sort of proof that bigfoot exists, they'd finally leave me alone.

"Do you have any idea how hard it is being the weirdo? Do you have any clue what it's like hearing people say things about your parents? And I don't mean now that you've got saddled with me as your only friend. I mean before all that when you were Little Miss Popular." He pauses for a moment, looking at me as though waiting for an answer to his rhetorical question and I can't meet his gaze. "No," he continues when I don't answer. "You don't know. You'll never know what it's like to be that lonely. To be so desperate that you'd risk your life going out in the middle of the forest just to make it stop."

The silence that envelopes the room after Simon stops speaking is thick with tension. He's still sitting next to me on the bean bag chair, our bodies touching as the soft material forces us to meet in the center. But even with his knee pressed against mine, I feel like he's a million miles away from me. I need to fix this. Simon is the only friend I've got and I feel like an idiot for pushing him away. I can't lose him. Not now. Not with Carissa and Kate on the brink of killing me. Not with that anonymous message looming over my head, reminding me that there's someone else out there who knows. Someone else out there who wants to hurt me.

I lean forward and take Simon's hand, gripping it tight when he tries to pull away so he's forced to stay in my grasp.

"Simon, please," I beg him. "I really am sorry. For all of it. I shouldn't have said those things just now and I shouldn't have done what I did that night. It was stupid and childish and I regret it every single day since it's happened. You think I don't know what it's like to be desperate, but I do. I'd do anything to take back what I did. I'd risk anything to at least find that thing we saw and prove to everyone that I'm not crazy. That *we're* not crazy. Why do you think I agreed to do the podcast with you in the first place? It's not just because of what we saw. I want answers just as much as you do. Because maybe if I find them, I can at least make some of it right. I can at least give the Popes some answers instead of them having to sit there and wonder for all these years what really happened to their daughter."

Simon keeps his eyes trained on our hands as they remain clasped together in his lap. His cheeks turn pink and my throat constricts when I realize what might be running through his mind. I clear my throat and release my grip on his hand, ignoring the butterflies as they beat their wings relentlessly against my stomach lining. Simon isn't a bad-looking guy. I mean, he's no Joel Baker, but he's kind of cute in his own quirky, Daniel-Radcliffe-as-Harry-Potter sort of way. But he's my best friend—or at least, he used to be before I opened my mouth about all this mess. I don't want to ruin things even more by complicating our relationship. I've never even thought about him in that way. But the way his face makes the full transformation from light pink to bright red when I drop his hand back in his lap tells me that he has thought about it.

And now I feel even worse.

"Why didn't you tell me sooner?" His question breaks the strangled silence between us and I try to sit a little taller in the bean bag sofa, but the more I try, the more the material swallows me up.

"I just couldn't," I admit. "I was scared. I'm still scared. And now Carissa and Kate think I told somebody, and they're going to kill me for it. I just know it."

"Wait, why do they think you told somebody after all this time?" My stomach flips when Simon asks the question and I realize that I still haven't told him the most important part of my story. He senses that I'm holding back and pushes for a response, "C'mon, E. I know you're hiding something else. Might as well just spill the beans."

The tightness in my chest loosens a bit when he calls me E. He's already forgiven me... sort of. It gives me the courage to tell him what else is on my mind.

"You remember this morning at my locker?"

"You mean when you ran out of school like you were being chased by a Sasquatch?" Simon smirks. "Yeah, I remember."

"Well, I ran because I was scared," I admit. Simon tilts his head, confusion written all over his face as he looks at me.

"Scared of what?"

"What I found in my locker." The words are barely above a whisper as they leave my lips. Before Simon can ask for clarification, I explain to him about the Fix-A-Flat. The photo of Renée. The handwritten note beneath her portrait.

I know what you did.

"Carissa and Kate got the same thing in their lockers," I add. "But they wouldn't listen to me when I told them that I got a note, too. Just told me I was lying and threatened to beat me up. But I'm scared, Si. Someone else knows what we did, and I'm afraid of what they might do."

He's quiet for a long time after I finish telling him everything, and when he finally speaks, his voice is filled with worry.

"I don't like the sound of this," he says. "We need to tell somebody."

"I can't tell anybody," I protest. "I'll be in so much trouble if I do."

"E, this is serious." Simon levels me with a look that reminds me of Dad whenever he goes into Full Parent Mode. "Whoever left you guys that note isn't messing around. What if they try to hurt you? What if they try to—"

"I know." I cut him off before he voices the fears that have been clawing at my brain all day. "I know it's dangerous. But I can't do it, Si. I can't tell anybody else about what we did that night. You remember what the police said: Whoever slashed the tires is Renée's killer. If they found out we're the ones who did it, what do you think they're going to do to us?"

"Oh, c'mon." Simon waves his hand through the air like I'm being ridiculous. "You really think the cops are gonna believe that a group of middle schoolers killed a high school senior in the woods one night for no reason?"

"Why not?" I challenge him. "You remember that episode we did about Slenderman? How those girls in Wisconsin stabbed their classmate to death? They were only twelve years old at the time—a whole year younger than we were. Who's to say we couldn't have done it? It's easier to believe that than the truth. You're the only person who saw what I saw that night. You think the police will believe us if we try to tell them that a Sasquatch did it? They'd laugh right in our faces while they put me in handcuffs. No. No way. We're not going to *anyone* about this."

Simon stays quiet. He knows I'm right. No good will come from going to an adult about this. The best thing to do is keep quiet and hope that whoever sent those notes isn't as serious as we think they are.

A few moments pass and Simon looks around the room until his gaze lands on the digital clock hanging above the computer desk where all the podcast equipment is out, still waiting for us to produce this week's episode. The episode about Renée. I wonder if Simon still wants to do it. If he still thinks interviewing Asher Pope is a good idea for the festival. As if reading my mind, he turns to me and clears his throat.

"It's seven o'clock," he announces. "It's getting late. Let's just skip the show this week, okay?"

I let out a sigh of relief and nod my head. "Okay. That sounds good."

"C'mon." Simon hoists himself up from the bean bag chair and extends his hand to help me up. "I'll walk you home."

"I can't," I tell him as I take his hand and allow him to pull me up to a standing position. "My mom's car is still at the trailhead. I can't just leave it there."

"Okay, well, there's no way I'm letting you walk all the way out there by yourself. The sun's set already. It'll be pitch dark in the woods by this point. Let me see if I can borrow my mom's car or something."

I nod and thank him for the offer, grateful that I won't have to brave the forest alone at night for a second time. Together, we leave the garage behind and head back to the main house. I stay on the front porch while Simon runs inside to ask his mom for her car keys. Before I know it, we're piling into her little blue Toyota Corolla that's parked in the garage bay below the loft where we just were.

It's a six-minute drive to the trailhead from Simon's house, but the silence in the car makes it feel like six hours. I know it's a good sign that he didn't just leave me to fend for myself and hike through the forest alone, but I can't help feeling like things are different between us now. And not just because of the awkwardness that came from holding his hand.

Why did I do that?

The memory forces me to keep my gaze fixed on the blinding darkness drifting by the car window rather than on Simon's concentrated expression as he navigates through the shadowy trees that surround us. As I turn my attention to the forest, my breath catches in my throat and before I know it, I'm reaching for Simon's hand yet again.

"E, what're you—"

"Si." The whisper comes out hoarse and frantic as it leaves my lips. It's all I can say as I crane my neck, eyes wide with fear while I struggle to locate what I know I just saw stomping through the trees.

"E, you're freaking me out," Simon says. "I'm pulling over."

"No!" I shout and the sound causes Simon to press down harder on the gas pedal. "Don't stop the car. There's... there's something out there."

A chill runs down my spine as tears burn at the back of my eyes.

Please, God, not again.

"What do you mean there's something out there?" Simon's gaze is fixed on the road, but I still see the fear in his face as I turn to look at him. It's not a real question. He already knows the answer.

"Just get me to my mom's car so we can get the hell out of here," I urge. "Hurry up. I'm freaking out."

"Oh, yeah, like this is *so* fun for me," Simon barks out a bitter laugh. "What did you see?"

"I... I don't know how to explain it," I stammer. "It just looked like a person walking, but it was too—"

"Hairy? Big?" Simon guesses.

"Exactly." My confirmation sends a wave of goosebumps over my arms. "We need to get out of here. Fast."

"Okay just... hang on." Simon presses down on the gas a little harder and the branches whiz by the car at breakneck speed as we zoom along the dirt road to the gravel lot at the edge of South Bay. The Corolla's headlights flood the tiny parking area, casting a yellow spotlight on my mom's orange Beetle. But there's something else in the parking lot, too, and the moment I see it, I almost throw up from the pain as my insides twist. And I'm not the only one who finds the discovery disturbing. Simon casts a nervous glance in my direction.

"Is that Carissa's car?"

Crap.

As if it wasn't terrifying enough to have seen that *thing* marching out there in the woods, now I have to worry that Carissa and Kate are trying to ambush me so they can wrap up their unfinished business. Have they been waiting for me to come back all this time? Are they sitting in the car right now, planning their attack? My knees start to tremble at the thought. I don't know what's worse: dying at the hands of a Sasquatch or getting torn to shreds by the two girls who hate me the most.

Simon brings the car to a stop about ten feet from Mom's Beetle and Carissa's glitzy Mercedes. The high beams are on, and the bright light makes it easy to see that there's no one sitting inside either vehicle. At first, the realization comforts me. But no sooner does relief flood my system than it drains from my body in an instant as I'm forced to ask an even more terrifying question.

If Carissa isn't inside her car, then where is she?

There's no time for me to sit here and try to figure it out. That thing is still out there, and if we don't get out of here fast, Simon and I are going to be the next kids to turn up dead in the woods.

"I'm going to the car," I tell him. "Don't leave until I get it started."

"Of course not, are you crazy? I'd never do that to you." Simon licks his lips nervously as I reach for the door handle and step out of the car. "Be careful, E. And hurry."

I slam the car door behind me and race to the Beetle, thankful for the warm glow of the Corolla's headlights as I fumble with the keys and slip inside the driver's seat. As I insert the keys into the ignition, I say a silent prayer that the engine starts without issue. It hadn't given me any trouble at all earlier. But of course as I twist the keys in the ignition, all I hear is the whining stutter as the starter fails to turn over and bring the engine to life.

"C'mon, c'mon, c'mon," I plead with the car to comply with my wishes. I try for a second time. A third. On the fourth attempt, the engine purrs to life and I think I might cry from relief. The firing of pistons through the aging motor is the most beautiful sound I've ever heard. I honk the horn to let Simon know that I'm good to go, and he gets the message. Before long, we're speeding back down the same road we just traveled with Simon leading the way while I trail him from behind, my front bumper mere inches from his tailgate like I'm trying to push him faster down the road. I can't help it. The thought of falling too far behind and getting trapped in the darkness with that beast terrifies me more than anything.

Within minutes, we're through the trees and back in the heart of town. Simon carves a path through the darkened streets until he arrives outside my house and I park Mom's car in the driveway. I get out of the driver's seat and walk down to the sidewalk on shaky legs, my heart still racing with adrenaline as I lean in through the passenger's side window that Simon rolls down for me as I approach the Corolla.

"Thanks for going with me," I say. "If it weren't for you, I'd probably be dead right now."

"No problem," he mutters, and my heart sinks at the tone of his voice. He's still mad at me.

"I guess you hate me now, huh?" My voice wobbles around the words and I have to bite down on my lip to keep from sobbing. Simon breathes out a long, heavy sigh.

"No, E, I don't hate you," he says. "I could never hate you, you know that. I just... don't hide stuff from me anymore, okay? Promise me you won't do that anymore."

"I promise," I tell him.

And I mean it. I really do.

Chapter 10

I wake up having a panic attack. My chest hurts from how hard my heart is thumping against my ribcage. There's this annoying ringing in my ears that's only adding to the headache I feel from all the pressure built up around my temples. All I can think about is that horrible nightmare, those glowing red eyes still burned into my retinas even as I blink away the last remnants of sleep. An awful sinking feeling cements itself in my bones, and it's not just because I died again in my dream last night. It's because even though I was the one feeling all the pain in my abdomen as that monster tore out my guts, it wasn't my body being ripped to pieces in the passenger seat of that strange car. It wasn't me at all living out my nightmare.

It was Carissa.

I swing my legs over the edge of my bed and race out my bedroom door to make my way to the bathroom. A hazy yellow glow fills the room when I flip the light switch and head over to the dusty mirror hanging above the bathroom sink. Relief surges through me as I take in my reflection, happy to see that contrary to what my dreams might want me to believe, this isn't *Freaky Friday* and I didn't trade places with my high school bully overnight. There's no head full of bleach-blonde locks staring back at me. No blue eyes or plump, pink lips or perfectly tanned skin. Just a mop of chestnut brown hair streaked with faded pink dye and gray-blue eyes rimmed red with sleep exhaustion confirming that I'm still me. I'm still Eliza Loft.

And I'm still probably going to get my butt kicked in school today.

"E, get a move on!" Dad's voice booms down the hallway from the staircase. "You're gonna be late, Little Foot!"

I splash a handful of cold water on my face, allowing the freezing liquid to jolt me into full consciousness and erase the memories of that haunting nightmare from my mind. This day is going to be bad enough as it is. I don't need some stupid dream taking up space in my head on top of it all.

"I'll be ready in a second!" I holler back to Dad and the proclamation sends fresh panic through my veins. I wonder how long Carissa and Kate will wait before attacking me. Will I have time to make it into the school building? Or will they corner me in the parking lot and beat me senseless before I can even reach the push handle to the double glass entrance? Maybe if I show up late enough, they won't beat me up at all. Oh, who am I kidding? If that happens, they'll just wait until the end of the school day to issue whatever punishment they have in store. Showing up late will just delay the inevitable.

No matter what I do, I'm a goner.

After brushing my teeth and my hair, I head back to my bedroom and change into a pair of black, fleece-lined leggings and a dark purple sweater dress. Might as well look cute if I'm going to die today. I grab my phone off my nightstand and my backpack off my desk chair, then bound downstairs to meet Dad in the kitchen.

"You know, your phone *does* have an alarm feature." He smirks at me as I join him at the counter, his fingers nimbly folding aluminum over what I'm certain is another bacon, egg, and cheese sandwich judging from the intoxicating aroma wafting through the room. Dad gives me a quick once-over, a quizzical brow arching over his green eyes as he takes me in. "What's the matter? Funnybone got twisted in your sleep?"

I peel my lips back into a tight line that I hope resembles enough of a smile that it'll put Dad's worried mind to rest. He can't know how scared I am to go to school today. If he does, he'll start to ask questions about why. Questions that I can't answer. Because then he'll know what a terrible person his daughter truly is.

"Sorry," I mutter, accepting the sandwich as he hands it to me. "I'll program the alarm tonight, I promise."

He tousles my hair and I wriggle out from beneath his fingertips.

"C'mon, Dad," I grumble, smoothing down the strands of hair that he just disturbed with his gruff hands. He chuckles at my fussing and pulls me in for a hug before I have time to slink away.

"Need you again at the store today, Little Foot," he reminds me and I slap him on the chest with my open palm.

"Keep calling me that and you're gonna have to get someone else to help," I warn. I feel the laughter rumble through his chest before he finally releases me and I slip out of the kitchen to the foyer. Riley is too busy napping on the sofa to try and plant stinky kisses on my face while I lace up my sneakers this morning.

With a mountain of anxiety radiating through my body, I trudge down the steps of our front porch and pile into the driver's seat of Mom's Beetle. It seems I'm not the only one dreading going to school today. The car fights me every time I twist the keys in the ignition. For a moment, I think the failing engine might be the thing that saves me from my doom. But as soon as Dad starts climbing down the stairs to grab the jumper cables from the back of his pickup so he can give me a boost, the car comes alive and all my dreams are dashed.

A light drizzle splatters across the windshield as I putter through town, the dreary weather a perfect match for my downcast mood. The closer I get to Whitehall High, the more erratic my heartbeat becomes. By the time I select a spot to park the car and kill the ignition, I can feel my pulse behind my eyes. Little black spots dot the corners of my vision until it feels like I'm peering through a tunnel.

This is it, I think as I grab my backpack and breakfast sandwich off the passenger's seat. *It was nice knowing me.*

The rain is coming down harder now as I cross the parking lot and make a beeline for the front entrance. As I take shelter beneath the long, narrow overhang that juts out from the school's entryway, a thick droplet of ice-cold rainwater splashes down my neck. *Perfect.* Like I need another excuse to feel uncomfortable this morning. I let out a sigh that's equal parts apprehension and aggravation as I push through the glass doors and make my way inside the building to face my fate.

Here goes nothing.

My stomach drops when I enter the lobby, but not because I walk in to find a rowdy group of students waiting to watch me get my butt kicked. On the contrary, the halls are so quiet, it's the absence of sound that raises the hairs on the back of my arms. Students huddle together in solemn clusters, grave expressions on their faces that only add to the feeling of unease building in my stomach as I pass them on my way to my locker. I strain my ears, trying to overhear the hushed whispers that spill from the lips of my peers behind their cupped hands, but the squeak of my wet sneakers against the linoleum is all I can hear.

When I round the corner to the hallway containing my locker, I'm unsurprised to see Simon is already standing there waiting for me. What does surprise me, however, is the sight of Joel Baker crouched against the wall outside the boys' restroom. His knees are hugged to his chest, his head nestled in the tight cocoon he's formed from his arms that are folded over the top of his legs. As I inch closer to him, I can see his shoulders shaking, can hear this mournful whimper muffled beneath the sleeves of his leather letterman jacket as he sobs in front of the entire school.

What the heck is going on?

I crane my neck around, wondering why no one is coming to ask him what's the matter. Doesn't anyone care that Whitehall High's star quarterback is crying in a corner outside the bathroom? It doesn't appear so. Everyone seems too busy spreading gossip to pay the sobbing athlete any mind. Before I can stop myself, I bend down next to him and place a gentle hand on his quaking shoulder.

"Joel? What's going on? Are you hurt or something?" A guttural sob erupts from his throat, and I have to focus all my attention on maintaining my balance to keep from toppling over at the noise. Pins and needles tingle along my arms and legs as I'm reminded of the day Mom died. How Dad sounded like a deer left for dead in the woods when the doctors came to meet us in the waiting room, shaking their heads as they told us there was nothing else they could do. When Joel lifts his head from his makeshift shelter, I swear I see my dad's face staring back at me. His curly brown hair sticks to his forehead, his usual bronze complexion replaced with pallid skin that makes me think of corpses. The sight of him alone is enough to make me want to shed tears of my own.

"Sh-she's g-gone." His voice cracks when he says the words, and I almost don't understand what he's said. But once it hits me, an arctic chill settles in the center of my gut.

"Who's gone?" I press him cautiously. His bloodshot blue eyes flood with fresh tears as his lips tremble, struggling to form the words. He breaks down before he can say anything, so I'm forced to ask him again. "Joel, talk to me. What happened? Who's gone?"

Before I know what's happening, Joel flings his arms around me and buries his face into the crook of my neck. I can't help the surge of excitement that flows through me as we cling to each other. I've wanted to be this close to Joel Baker for as long as I can remember. But even as I hug him to my chest and rub the space between his shoulder blades, I know this isn't right. And what he says next confirms it. My heartbeat stutters in my chest when the words reach my ears.

"Wh–what did you say?" I ask him to repeat it because I don't want to believe it's true. He pulls away and shudders as he sucks in a deep breath, his face shiny with tears still spilling down his cheeks.

"Carissa," he whispers. "She's... dead."

I can't hear the bell to first period over the sound of the ringing in my ears.

The school day drifts by in slow motion, and I catch myself pinching at my skin every so often just to make sure that I'm awake. That this isn't some hyper-realistic continuation of my nightmare. But no matter how hard I dig my fingernails into my flesh, I don't wake up.

Because this is real.

"They found her body in the woods this morning!"

"She went out for a hike and never came home."

"They found her car at the trailhead."

"The police don't have any leads on the killer."

Carissa's death is the only topic of discussion that fills the halls as I move from class to class. As I overhear each fresh take on the same story, I'm reminded of the day Renée's body was discovered. The similarities are so striking, it only amplifies the feeling that I'm living out some terrible dream. But the overwhelming sensation of déjà vu isn't even the worst part. What makes my stomach churn with acid isn't the knowledge that Carissa suffered the same fate as Renée and that poor girl up by Saranac Lake. It's the fact that even though I know it's wrong on so many levels, some small part of me feels relieved that she's gone.

I'm so ashamed of myself, I almost skip pre-calculus just to avoid seeing Carissa's empty desk mocking me with her absence. But I don't ditch class, so when I enter Mr. Atkins's room and my eyes land on the void where

Carissa's body used to be, it steals my breath away. I'm so focused on her absence that I almost don't realize that someone else is missing from the room as well. When it finally hits me, I feel dizzy with dread.

Where is Kate?

"Alright, class, listen up." Mr. Atkins interrupts my thoughts with his stern teacher voice and I snap my head to the front of the room rather than continue fixating on Kate's empty desk. "I know today is difficult for many of you, and I want to express my deepest condolences to those of you who are suffering after this tremendous loss. Please join me in taking a moment of silence to honor Carissa's memory."

A hush falls over the room, the only sounds those of the poorly stifled sobs that hiccup from the mouths of a few students. After a solid minute of silence, Mr. Atkins clears his throat, a pained expression on his face as he gushes about how deeply missed Carissa will be and what a positive impact she had on all of our lives. I have to bite down on my tongue to keep from laughing at the remark.

Be nice, Eliza, I chastise myself. *It doesn't matter that she was evil. A girl is dead. Have some respect.*

I do my best to focus on Mr. Atkins's math lesson, but my gaze keeps drifting back to Carissa's empty seat. It's not just me who's struggling to pay attention. On multiple occasions, my eyes lock with one classmate or another who can't seem to keep from staring at the vacant desk. It's like the seat is a magnet and our eyes are bits of scrap metal that can't escape its pull. Each time one of us looks away, another cranes their neck to stare and wonder, *What happened to her?* Then an even more horrifying thought: *Will it happen to me, too?*

Before long, the bell rings and class is over. As I stand up to exit the room and proceed to English class, my eyes linger on the empty desks where Carissa and Kate would normally be there to mock me. Though I understand why Carissa's remains empty, I'm still wondering why Kate isn't there to occupy her seat. Was she just too sad and overwhelmed to come to school today? Or is there something more sinister going on? My insides twist at the notion as I'm reminded once again of the note we all received in our lockers yesterday morning.

I know what you did.

I gulp down the bile stinging at the back of my throat as terrifying thoughts run rampant through my head. What if Carissa was killed by whoever left that note? What if Kate was killed, too, and the park rangers just haven't found her body yet?

What if I'm next?

I'm so stricken with fear that I barely register Simon's terse greeting as I sink into the empty desk beside him when I arrive at our English class.

"Have a nice morning with Joel?" he snarks. Heat rushes to my face as a violent combination of anger and embarrassment colors my cheeks red.

"I was comforting him," I snap. "His girlfriend just died, for crying out loud, Si. Have a little compassion, would ya?"

Simon scoffs.

"Please," he mutters. "Like you actually care that she's dead."

"What the heck is that supposed to mean?" I shoot back. Simon refuses to look at me, busying himself by thumbing through the pages of *Ethan Frome* until he finds the spot where we left off in class the previous day.

"Forget it," he grumbles. I don't understand why he's being such a jerk to me right now. Even if he is still holding a grudge about the secret I kept, I don't know what that has to do with the fact that Carissa is dead aside from the possibility that she was targeted because of what we did. Simon is my best friend. Shouldn't he be worried for me instead of holding onto the fact that I kept the truth hidden from him all these years? Just as I open my mouth to give him a piece of my mind, I stop myself short. Because it's in this moment that I realize the real reason Simon is being so spiteful.

He's jealous. And even though I have no reason to feel this way, knowing that he's jealous makes me feel a little guilty.

"Simon, look, I—"

"Good afternoon, class." An unfamiliar voice cuts me off before I can get the rest of the words out. I turn to face the front of the room and find a short, stout woman with blue, bedazzled cat-eye glasses blinking back at me. "I'm Mrs. Connors and I'll be filling in for Mr. Pope today. He's feeling a little under the weather but should be back in time for class tomorrow. Now, please open up your books to page sixty-eight."

The sound of turning pages fills the room as students rush to open their books, eager to have a distraction from the solemnity of the day. But all I can think about is Asher Pope and whether he really is sick, or if his sudden illness has more to do with the fact that another girl turned up dead in the same woods where his sister was found years earlier.

Chapter II

It's Tuesday and almost an entire week has passed since Carissa's death, but Kate still hasn't shown up for school. Every day when I head to pre-calculus, I convince myself that she'll be there. And every day when I show up, her desk is still empty. No one has said anything about it; Carissa is the only thing on anybody's mind these days. And even though I'm certain that I would have heard about it by now if something had happened to Kate, there's a small seed of doubt rooted in my chest that grows bigger and bigger with each day that passes in her absence. Because if Kate is hurt (or worse), I know it's only a matter of time until I'm next.

As if the thought of being targeted by some deranged psychopath isn't bad enough, Simon and I have barely spoken since news of Carissa's death started spreading. We're supposed to do the podcast episode today that we skipped last week, but he hasn't mentioned it once, which is so unlike him. Plus, we have the festival next weekend and we still haven't nailed down who our guest is going to be for the live show. I know he said he didn't hate me the night he helped me pick up my car at the trailhead, but it's starting to feel like maybe he does.

As my mind ping-pongs between Carissa's death and Kate's absence, I find myself thinking about holding hands with Simon in his bean bag chair and how a gesture so small could have an impact this big on our friendship. I didn't think anything could make me feel as much regret as I did after slashing Renée Pope's tires, but the memory of Simon's hand in mine gives me that same guilty feeling. It's not like I find him repulsive or anything. In fact, the more I think about it, the more I have to admit to myself that I kind of liked it. Sort of. Maybe. Whatever. That's not the point, and it doesn't matter anyway. The only thing that matters is I miss my friend, and I'm tired of him pulling away from me when I need him most. I'm scared and I'm lost and I'm so freaking lonely that I can't even stand it. If things don't go back to the way they were soon, I feel like I'm going to scream.

Be the bigger person, E, I can hear Mom's voice ringing in my ears as I slide into the empty desk next to Simon's when I get to English class. Even though she's dead and I know the voice isn't real, I also know she's right. So, I suck it up and I do it. I act like the bigger person.

"Hey," I say to Simon as I sink into my seat. He grunts in my direction and I roll my eyes. "Si, c'mon. Stop torturing me already. Please? I miss you."

"Why don't you go hang out with Joel?" he mumbles.

"Oh my goodness, how long are you gonna hang onto that? Nothing even happened. I was just trying to be nice and we haven't said two words to each other since. He doesn't even think of me that way."

"Do you?" Simon asks.

"Do I what?"

"Think of him that way?"

"Simon..." I pinch the bridge of my nose in frustration and let out a sigh.

"Just answer the question," Simon demands, and I swear if his face wasn't inches out of my reach, I'd slap it. He's being so childish right now. It's all I can do to keep from shouting at him.

"Yes," I hiss, but then I see the hurt in Simon's eyes and I instantly regret it. "I mean no. Crap. I don't know. It doesn't even matter, okay? In case you haven't noticed, I've got more important things to think about than who I do or don't have a crush on. Like the fact that Carissa's dead, Kate's missing, and I'm probably going to be the next one to turn up dead if those stupid notes in our locker have anything to do with all this mess."

I slam my hands on my desk and fold my arms across its surface before sinking my head down on top. Why does everything and everyone have to be so difficult? Why can't I just have a normal life? And why can't I seem to get through a single day anymore without breaking down into a puddle of tears?

As the saltwater rolls down my nose and drips onto my desk, I feel a bony hand wrap around my shoulder.

"E, I… I'm sorry," Simon says. "I shouldn't have been such a jerk to you. I guess I just… I don't know. Never mind. Like you said, it doesn't matter."

I wipe the tears away on the back of my sleeve as I pick my head up and face him. "It's fine." I sniffle. "Let's just forget it, okay? Truce?"

"Truce." Simon's lips quirk upward and I feel myself return a smile despite it all. "So, you ready for the show?"

And just like that, we're friends again like nothing ever happened. My shoulders sag as I laugh out a sigh of relief. "You know it," I answer. "Except maybe we steer clear of the Renée story—just until everything calms down."

"What? No way! We have to do it now," Simon protests. "The festival is next week and we have to get Asher to agree to the live show. If we don't do the story on Renée—"

"Simon and Eliza!" Mr. Pope's voice cracks like a whip through the air and our spines stiffen in unison. When we turn to face the front of the room, Mr. Pope glowers back at us. The anger coming from his eyes is so palpable, I can practically feel my skin burn from the heat of his stare. His voice is like thunder when he speaks again, "Is there something that you'd like to share with the rest of the class?"

"N–no, Mr. Pope," I stammer.

"Then I suggest you both be quiet," he snaps. "Unless, of course, you'd like detention after school today?"

Scarlet splotches sneak their way up my neck until I can feel the warmth spread across my cheeks as a chorus of *ooohs* echoes through the room. Mr. Pope shushes his students, but it doesn't matter. I'm mortified, and even though I refuse to look over at him to confirm it, I know Simon is, too. We keep our focus on the lesson, not daring to even glance in each other's direction until the bell rings and class is finally over. Even then, we wait until we're in the safety of the hallway to speak to one another.

"Well, *that* was embarrassing," I groan as we snake our way through the crowd to find the cafeteria.

"Hope he doesn't hate us too much," Simon laments. "We need to get on his good side if he's gonna be on our show. There's not much time left to ask him to do it."

"I don't know, Si." I shake my head, trying to erase the image of Mr. Pope's angry eyes from my mind. Something about the way he looked at us felt... personal. Like we weren't just chatty students disrupting his class. Like there was something more to it. I think about the first day he introduced himself as our substitute and the way he looked at me then and I shudder. "There's something... off about him, don't you think?"

"What do you mean?" Simon grabs a tray from the pile stacked at the end of the lunch line as we join the queue of students waiting to receive their meals. I lower my voice as we continue our conversation, not wanting to be overheard by our peers.

"I mean there's something about him that rubs me the wrong way. The way he looks at me sometimes, it's like he... like he knows." I catch Simon's eye when I say it, hoping he understands my unspoken meaning. The corners of his mouth sink into a frown as his brows knit together across his forehead.

"What are you saying?" I bite down on the inside of my cheek as I consider his question. The truth is, I don't really know what I'm saying. All I know is that I get a strange feeling in my gut whenever Mr. Pope looks at me, and the last thing I want to do is make him hate me even more by trying to get him to talk about his dead sister.

"I don't know what I'm saying," I admit. "Maybe I'm just reading into it too much. Ever since this whole thing with Carissa, I just feel like I've always gotta be looking over my shoulder. And Kate still isn't in school…"

"Yeah, where is she anyway?" Simon selects a slice of pepperoni pizza from beneath the heat lamp and adds it to his tray while I choose a slice of plain pie. I shrug, ripping a piece of pepperoni off his slice and popping it into my mouth. "Hey!" He nudges me playfully in the arm. "Get your own!"

I crinkle my nose and stick out my tongue, putting the chewed-up pepperoni on full display.

"You're so nasty," Simon remarks and we burst out laughing. Despite all the horrible things that have happened in the past week, all the awkwardness that had taken up space between us, it feels good to share a laugh. To pretend like things are normal even though it sometimes feels like nothing will ever be normal again.

We continue down the line and pay for our food, emerging from the queue together as we scan the cafeteria to find an empty seat. There's a table at the far end of the room beside the double doors that lead out to the courtyard in the back of the school. Aside from the group of artsy types sitting together at one end, the rest of the table is up for grabs, so we take a seat before anyone can steal it away from us. After taking a few bites of our pizza, Simon starts the conversation back up.

"You didn't answer me before." I tilt my head in confusion and he rolls his eyes. "About Kate, dummy," he teases. "Where do you think she is?"

My eyes drift to the table in the center of the room where Carissa and Kate would normally be seated among the crowd of popular kids who are all there currently eating together, munching away on their meals like there aren't two members of their tribe obviously missing.

"I don't know where she is," I confess. "She hasn't been in school since it happened."

"Do you think she's just...grieving?" Simon guesses and I bump my shoulders, swallowing another bite of pizza before providing a verbal response.

"I really don't know, but it worries me that she's been out this long," I tell him. "I mean, I get it. They were best friends. I'd be a mess if I lost you. But I wasn't even out a full week after my mom... after she... anyway, I just feel like there's something else going on. There's something more to it."

Simon nods his head, chewing for longer than I feel is necessary to grind up the small bite of pizza I just watched him pop into his mouth. But I get it. Whenever I bring up Mom's death, I can tell it makes him uncomfortable. Maybe not *uncomfortable*. But he definitely feels at a loss for words. Like he's terrified he'll say the wrong thing and I'll start uncontrollably sobbing or something. Finally, he swallows and offers up a suggestion.

"Have you tried calling her or texting her or anything?" I bark out an ironic laugh.

"You think I still have her number after everything that happened between us? No way. Even if I did, I doubt she'd answer me if I tried to call. *If* she's even around to answer."

"Hey, don't talk like that," Simon chastises me. "You don't know what the deal is. For all we know, she could just be at home. You know what? I bet that's *exactly* where she is. We should go there."

I cough on the cola I just chugged, nearly spitting it across the table when he says the words. "Are you nuts?" I choke. The thought of showing up unannounced together on Kate Richards's doorstep would make me laugh if it weren't so terrifying.

"Look, you want answers, don't you?" I pause, considering the question, then nod when I have to admit that answers are the only thing that I want right now. They're the only thing that has even the smallest chance of making me feel better about any of this. "So, do you want to sit here and wallow, or do you want to get the answers you need?"

I tilt my head back and grunt at the ceiling. "Fine," I groan out as the dread pools in my stomach, thoughts of standing on Kate's front porch while she screams in my face already making my insides burn. "But if I'm gonna do this, I think I should go alone. If she is at home and she knows more about what happened to Carissa, she'll never tell me about it if you're there. No offense."

"None taken." Simon puts up his hands, deflecting any hidden hurt he might feel from the words I've just said.

"Well, I guess I know where I'm headed after school today." I gulp.

"Don't sweat it." Simon waves his hand through the air like he's swatting away my worries, but the action doesn't do anything to calm my nerves. He senses my lingering tension and places his hand over mine, giving it a soft squeeze. "You'll be fine," he assures me. "And even if you're not, I'll be there for you after it's all done."

"Promise?"

"Cross my heart." He removes his hand from mine and traces an "X" across his chest. I'm grateful when he doesn't say, *Hope to die.*

Chapter 12

It's been years since I last climbed the stone steps that lead to Kate's massive front porch. Tucked away at the end of a cul-de-sac on the edge of West Mountain, the Victorian manor is one of only ten such properties belonging to the lucky few families who enjoy their status as Whitehall's wealthier residents. Not that luck has much to do with Kate's upper-class upbringing. From what I recall of the few heart-to-hearts we shared before our falling out, nothing of her privileged lifestyle was handed to her on a silver platter.

Despite the ivory columns and spiral staircase and stained-glass windows and gleaming hardwood floors, I always felt a little sorry for Kate. Of the four thousand people living in our little town, I can think of seven residents who belong to the Black community aside from her—three of whom are members of her family. Apart from Carissa's remarks about Kate's Jamaican mother, I never heard any of the other kids at school speak ill of her ethnicity. But even though I never heard anyone put Kate down for looking a little different than most other residents in town, I could still detect a lingering tension lying dormant within her. Like being rich enough to live in a manor on a hill in a town full of White folks somehow made her less Black.

"No one really says anything about it here—at least not to your face," she had told me once. "But back in the city, the kids at school used to tease me constantly for it. They would talk about my dad being White and all, making it out to be like my mom was just using him for money or something. But *she's* the one with the big, important job. And how is any of that *my* fault anyway? It's not like I asked for this."

I didn't ask her to elaborate on any of it. As a middle-class White girl growing up in the rural mountains of New York, I didn't feel I had much to offer in the way of wisdom when it came to issues of race. I just shut up and listened and tried my best to understand where she was coming from. That's what friends are for, no matter what their background happens to be. That's what Mom always said anyway.

Still, I had to admit that it did make sense why the other kids in school might've held feelings of prejudice toward Kate, though not for the color of her skin. If anything, it was her parents' wealth that made her a target. In Whitehall, the more backwoods and "real country" you are, the more friends you'll have. Maybe that's why I was embraced as the leader of our little group; my family never had much aside from the shop, so no one ever viewed me as an outsider. But Kate and Carissa? They always had more, and in a town where everyone has nothing, being the one person who has it all can end up losing you everything.

As I reach for the heavy, brass knocker on Kate's front door that looks like it was made for giants, a twinge of longing pinches at my heart. I love hanging out with Simon, and I'm grateful for our friendship. But I miss having a girlfriend to hang out with. Even though we came from such different backgrounds, I always got along great with Kate. She was funny and spunky and knew things about life that I could never hope to learn in my limited bubble of hiking trails and hunting seasons and sasquatch lore. The day she sided with Carissa and left me to fend for myself in a sea of laughing faces, I didn't blame her. I knew she was just doing what she needed to do, not just because of the pact we had made but because of all the things she told me about her struggles with fitting in, whether it was in the city or out here in the sticks. Still, it hurt to lose her as a friend. Much worse than it ever felt to lose Carissa.

Sometimes I wonder if she would have done it differently if given the chance. If she thinks about the way things used to be. If she misses me, too.

The sound of the rain drumming against the overhang that covers the front porch echoes so loud in my ears that I almost don't hear the click as Mrs. Richards unlocks the deadbolt and opens the door. A brightly colored tunic is draped around her torso, her long braids tied back in an equally bold-patterned head scarf. It's no wonder why the rich folks with fancy log cabins high up in the Adirondacks trust her to transform their interiors; she obviously has a knack for design. But the joyful array of colors and patterns that decorates her body doesn't seem to reach her face. Her dark eyes peer at me beneath a wrinkled brow, the corners of her wide mouth drawn down in a formidable scowl that gives me the sudden urge to run to the bathroom.

"Hi, Mrs. Richards, I'm—"

"I know who you are, child," she snaps. "What is it that you want?"

I don't need to look in a mirror to know that my cheeks are bright red. *This was a mistake*, I think as she stares me down. Her long lashes cast eerie shadows across her high cheekbones, making her appear even more menacing than her growling voice. For a moment, I consider leaving. It's clear that I'm not wanted here. But then I think about Carissa. I think about those notes in our locker. I think about what's going to happen to me if I don't figure out what's going on.

Screw it.

"Is Kate home?" I blurt. Just as Mrs. Richards opens her mouth to respond, a loud crash reverberates through the house behind her that sounds like an explosion of glass breaking across the floor.

"Mo-o-o-om!" Anthony yells out for his mother (or maybe it's Isaac—I could never tell the difference between the identical twins that Kate calls her younger brothers). Mrs. Richards rolls her eyes and mutters something that I don't understand but which I'm sure is some sort of Jamaican swear word under her breath. She closes the door halfway and hollers over her shoulder toward the sound of her whining son.

"Can't you two give me one *second* of peace?"

"But, Mom—"

"No, 'but, Mom.' I don't wanna hear nothin' about 'but, Mom.' Clean it up and I'll deal with you two later, y'understand me now?"

In a flash, she rips the door back open and the aggravation on her face is somehow even more shiver-inducing than it was when she first answered the door. She pinches the bridge of her nose and rubs the crease between her brows before turning her attention back to me.

"Now, what is it that you want? Hmm?" The way her eyes flash makes my throat go dry and I struggle to summon the words to speak. "Out with it, child!"

"I–I j–just wondered if Kate was home," I manage to say, and I hate the way my voice shakes as I say it. I'm not usually this bashful around adults (unless, of course, they're as devastatingly handsome as Mr. Atkins or as creepy and unsettling as Mr. Pope), but there's something about the way Mrs. Richards looks at me that makes me feel like a bumbling toddler too scared to ask her teacher for a box of crayons.

"Why?" It's a question, but the blunt edge of her voice makes it sound like an accusation.

"Well, she hasn't been in school since Carissa... since she... and I just was worried that maybe—"

"My daughter is none of your concern," she interrupts.

"But, Mrs. Richards, I'm scared that—"

"Didn't you hear me, child? This doesn't concern you. Now, I ask you, please, go." She makes a shooing motion with her hand and juts her chin toward the street, ushering me off her porch. I start to turn around, eager to get back to the safety of Mom's car after such a tense exchange, but just as I twist my torso to face the rain-spattered street, Mrs. Richards stops me again.

"And Liza?" My stomach drops at the sound of my nickname. "Don't you come back here no more. Leave my daughter alone, y'understand me now?"

My eyes widen and my mouth turns to cotton. Before I can respond, she slams the door in my face and I'm left on the porch with nothing but the sound of the pouring rain.

What the heck was that about?

Even when we were friends, I never remember exchanging more than a few words with Mrs. Richards. During the few sleepovers we shared and nights spent around her dinner table, I always thought my time with Kate's family had been pleasant. But the way Mrs. Richards just practically pushed me off her front porch makes it seem like we have a history of unsavory encounters. Like I'm a problem child that she wishes her daughter never got involved with. It makes me wonder what Kate has told her about me.

When I get into the driver's seat of Mom's Beetle, I'm shaking both from the freezing rain soaking into my tee shirt and from the bitter words from Mrs. Richards still rattling around my brain. I'm grateful when the engine comes to life immediately and hot air rushes forth from the vents, sending a trail of pleasurable goosebumps up my arms as I thaw out my frozen fingertips in front of the heater. As the feeling returns to my hands, my gaze drifts beyond the windshield and lands on the window furthest to the right on the second story of Kate's home—the window to her bedroom. And even though it's raining and gray and my mind is still racing from my conversation with her mom, I know I'm not imagining it when I see Kate's face framed between the curtains.

Watching me.

Chapter 13

It's a short drive to the Bigfoot Museum across town, but the stark difference between the posh neighborhood I just left in the rearview and the ramshackle building with the giant sasquatch statue out front makes it feel like I just took a cross-country trip. We don't normally do the podcast here, but with only a week to spare until the festival, Simon's parents need all the help they can get to prepare. Who knows? They might need so much help that we don't even get to do the show at all. Or maybe that's just my wishful thinking because I really don't want to do an entire episode about what happened to Renée.

I park the car in the tiny gravel lot and run to the entrance of the small, cement building that looks more like an abandoned convenience store than a museum. As

I push through the glass door entrance, a loud, howling noise that reminds me of the monster from my nightmares echoes through the lobby. Even though I've heard the gimmicky bell chime a thousand times before, it never ceases to send a shiver down my spine when I hear it.

The museum doesn't have very much in the way of exhibits. It's just one large room with a single reception desk in the middle. Next to it is a cardboard cutout of a sasquatch with pamphlets that Mrs. Little made detailing the history of bigfoot in the Adirondacks. Along the white-painted walls is a collection of photographs depicting the elusive cryptid in varying degrees of clarity, each accompanied by a brief description of the eyewitness account from the person who took the photo. Most of them are from locals eager to share their stories, but there are few from out of state. One even came all the way from Tacoma, which I think is in Washington. I'm not sure. I probably should have paid attention more in geography class last year.

"Look what the Squatch dragged in," Mr. Little teases as he peers up at me from the reception desk in the center of the room. I grin in response and wave in his direction.

"Hey, Mr. Little, how's it going?"

"Busy, busy." He taps his pencil on the stack of papers on his desk. "You know how it is this time of year. Gotta contact all the vendors, make sure the radio spots are in order, get the generators set up and whatnot... I wish there were two of me."

"Oh, what? I'm not enough help, is that what you're saying?" Mrs. Little sneaks up behind her husband as she exits the office at the back of the museum and plants a kiss on top of his bald spot. Simon trails behind her, shaking his head in embarrassment while his parents embrace, like the fact that they're still head-over-heels in love with each other after twenty years of marriage is too much for him to bear.

"Get a room, would ya?" he moans, joining me at my side. "C'mon, E, let's get out of here. Mom said we can use the office for the show."

"Yes, I did," Mrs. Little trills. She detangles herself from her husband just as he dives in for another kiss, missing her mouth and landing his lips on her cheek as she turns to face me and Simon. "But you have to help with the pamphlets afterward. That's the deal."

Simon rolls his eyes and grips my shoulders from behind, pushing me forward so we can escape his parents who are now gazing into each other's eyes like a scene out of some cheesy rom-com. I know he thinks it's lame, but I can't help but smile as we pass them. They remind me of the way my parents used to be when Mom was still alive.

Happy and jokey and totally in love. What I wouldn't give to catch them stealing kisses by the kitchen sink again. Sometimes it feels like those memories belong to someone else.

Once we get inside the office, Simon closes the door and leans against its surface, tilting his head back and wearing this withered expression like he can't believe the day he's having. He rakes his hands over his face and looks over at me with an apologetic smirk.

"Sorry about them," he mutters.

"Oh, I don't mind," I answer. "I think it's cute they still love each other so much. Hope I get to have that one day, don't you?"

Simon opens his mouth to respond but shuts it immediately. His cheeks are bright pink when he turns away and an awkward feeling hangs in the air between us. It's a small room with nothing but a wooden desk and a computer as ancient as the one in the back of Dad's general store, so there aren't many distractions I can lean on to dispel the tightness in my chest. I clear my throat, desperate to change the subject.

"Anyway... I went to Kate's house," I offer, hoping the statement will be enough to get rid of this terrible tension that is still somehow dominating every interaction we share. The color fades from Simon's face almost as quickly as it bloomed across his cheeks and he takes a seat on top of the computer desk. He kicks the rolling chair out from beneath the desk and gestures for me to take it, swinging his legs as they hover a few inches above the floor.

"So, what did you find out?" He looks at me expectantly. I take my seat and sigh.

"Not much," I confess. "Unless you count the fact that Kate's mom definitely hates me."

"*Hates* you?" Simon's eyes go wide and his nose crinkles, forcing his glasses to slide down to the tip of his hook nose. "Why do you think she hates you?"

I tell him all about the strange encounter I shared with Mrs. Richards and what her parting words were to me just before slamming the door in my face.

Leave my daughter alone.

Like I'm some sort of stalker who gets her kicks lurking outside of Kate's bedroom at night or something. When I finish telling Simon my story, he looks as shocked as I felt standing at Kate's doorstep.

"That's... weird," he decides.

"It gets weirder," I tell him. "After I got back to my car, I caught Kate staring at me from her bedroom window. She was just sitting there watching me. It was... creepy."

"So, you saw her, though? So, she's okay?"

"I mean, I guess she seemed alright from what I could see of her." I shrug. "I don't know. I guess I should be glad she's okay, but I still feel like there's something else going on. I mean, what the heck was that about with her mom? 'Leave my daughter alone.' Like I'm some sort of criminal or something!"

"Aren't you?" Simon waggles his eyebrows at me to let me know he's only joking, but I don't find it funny. My eyes flash with indignation and he throws his palms to the sky. "Sorry. Bad joke. Too soon. I get it."

"*Very* bad joke," I agree. It's quiet for a moment until Simon breaks the silence with a question that's been eating at my mind since the second I left Kate's house.

"Do you think her mom knows? About what happened, I mean?"

"I... don't know." I sink my teeth into my bottom lip. "It would be kind of stupid for her to tell, don't you think? I mean, what with everything going on with Carissa and all? If the cops think the same person who killed Renée is the one who killed Carissa, Kate would be implicating herself by telling her mom about what we did."

"But it wasn't a person who killed Renée," Simon reminds me. "Just like it wasn't a person who killed Carissa."

"How do you—"

"Did you hear about what happened to her? Like, what *really* happened to her?" Simon slides off the desk and turns around to face the computer screen before I have time to respond, jiggling the mouse to bring the machine to life.

"All I know is that she was found in the woods," I say. "You weren't talking to me all week, remember? I didn't get the full scoop."

"Oh, *whatever*." He waves his hand like I'm just making up excuses for my ignorance. "You act like you don't have access to the same message boards I do. It's all over the place! Check it out."

I roll the chair closer to the desk as Simon taps away at the keyboard to bring up the message board where all our fellow believers post about their latest cryptid encounters. He's right when he says I have access to the same forum, but if I'm being honest, I don't fully understand how it works. Every time I log on to the site, I feel like I'm staring at some old-school Word document that probably hasn't gotten a serious update since the time the internet was born, whenever that was. I've tried to get the hang of it, but I can never seem to find the things that Simon does, so I've learned to rely on him for any new information that makes its way to the board.

The website loads and fills the computer screen with its cream-colored background. At the top of the page is a logo of a hairy foot with the word "Big" on one side and "Believer" on the other. Even though the site is mainly geared towards Sasquatch sightings, people post about other things there sometimes as well. Like Chappy—Vermont's version of the Loch Ness Monster—or Slenderman or wendigo or skinwalkers. Just your average, everyday helping of firsthand encounters with entities that people refuse to acknowledge exist despite the fact that thousands of people have seen them. I'll admit there are some strange stories that even I have trouble believing. But the sheer volume of people out there who have had their lives turned upside down by something they couldn't explain is what keeps me coming back to it. I mean, we can't all be crazy—can we?

"Here it is," Simon announces when he finds the post he's been looking for. He turns to look at me and the excitement dims from his eyes, replaced with a look of concern. "I should warn you," he says slowly, "it's not pretty."

"I can handle it," I insist, hoping my voice sounds more confident than I feel. Deep down, though, I'm nervous. Visions of that beast tearing at Renée's body flood to the forefront of my mind. I can still hear the wet, suctional sound of blood spilling out of ripped flesh while Simon and I stood frozen in fear between the tall pines, waiting for the monster to finish its feast. It was bad enough to live through the first time when it was happening to someone I didn't know. But this was Carissa. Even though she had spent the past four years of our lives tormenting me at every opportunity and a small part of me was thankful to be rid of her, I still can't stomach the thought of her suffering a fate so grizzly. So gruesome. Do I really want to relive that moment? Do I really want to know what happened to the girl I used to call my friend?

Simon is still staring at me with that worried look in his eyes as I debate whether or not I want to confirm my worst fears. I know he doesn't mean anything by it, but it sparks this defiant energy in me like I need to prove to him that just because I'm a girl doesn't mean I'm any more of a wimp than he is. So, I scoot the chair closer to the computer screen and I start reading:

> **reelbigfoot19:** The monster is back in Whitehall. This time, a King was slain. He tore her limb from limb and tossed her torso in a bush. No one heard her screaming. But I did. I saw the whole thing. And it won't

be the last time. Because I'm always on the hunt.

By the time I finish reading, my jaw is on the floor. It's not as graphic as what Simon made it out to be, but there's something about the post that I find disturbing. I can't put my finger on why, but it makes me nervous—and I know it's not just because the poster is talking about a Sasquatch roaming the woods mere minutes away from where Simon and I are sitting in his parents' office.

"How do you know this is real?" I'm clinging to hope that this might be some sort of a hoax, but deep down I know that it isn't. If it were, Simon wouldn't have shown it to me. He's good about that stuff. He does his homework.

"My uncle is a park ranger, remember?" he reminds me. "He's the one who found her. He's not supposed to talk about that kind of stuff because of the police and all, but you know Uncle Scott. Loud mouth. I overheard him talking about it with my parents and he mentioned the thing about her torso, too. Said he had to pick twigs out of the spots where her—oh, sorry."

Simon stops talking when he sees the horrified expression on my face and I couldn't be more grateful to be spared from the gory details. I shake my head and squeeze my eyes shut, trying to clear away the images of Carissa's mangled corpse. When my eyelids flutter open, my gaze lands back on the post, those final words jumping out at me, demanding all of my attention.

And it won't be the last time. Because I'm always on the hunt.

"What do you think that means?" I point at the words on the screen and Simon leans in, his lips moving slightly as he reads.

"Probably just someone who knows what to look for, I'd guess." Simon shrugs it off like it's nothing, but I can't help feeling like there's more to it than that.

"Do you recognize this account? Have you seen them post to the forum before?" He rolls his eyes and shakes his head like he can't believe I could ask such a stupid question.

"Do you know how many stories get posted here each day, E? I can't keep track of every single user."

"Okay, well…is there a way we can find out if they've posted before? If they're 'always on the hunt,' then maybe they've seen some sort of pattern or something. Maybe they can help us. They might even be willing to do the live show!"

"You just don't want to interview Asher." Simon folds his arms and fixes me with an accusatory glare.

"That's not it at all," I lie. "But don't you think it'd be cool to have a Sasquatch hunter on the show? People would eat that up. And if they *can* help us find Bigfoot, we'd be heroes!"

Simon clicks his tongue and rubs his chin, mulling over the idea before nudging me out of the way so he can use the computer. With a few clicks of the mouse, he's somehow made it so only the posts from reelbigfoot19 populate the screen. There are three posts total: the one I just read, one dated July 20, 2023, and one dated September 9, 2019. When I see the date on the final post, my heart leaps out of my chest and I clap my hand over my mouth to keep from screaming.

"What? What's the matter?"

"That date," I whisper. "That's the day after Renée died."

Simon's eyes bulge out of his head and the two of us crowd the screen as we race to read the user's entry:

> **reelbigfoot19:** There's a monster in Whitehall. He killed the Pope girl last night. Ripped and ripped and ripped. No one heard her screaming. But I did. I saw the whole thing. And it won't be the last time. Because I'm always on the hunt.

Dread sinks like a stone in the pit of my stomach as an awful realization washes over me. When I turn to look at Simon, one look at his face is all I need to confirm that he's thinking the same thing.

"Do you remember seeing anyone else in the woods that night?" The words come out just above a whisper, but their significance sends this terrible ringing through my ears like a gunshot just went off. Because if the user was right about what happened to Carissa, then we have to believe what they say about Renée. But if we believe what they say about Renée, then it means Simon and I weren't the only ones who saw what happened to her. And if we weren't the only ones who saw it, I can think of only one explanation for why that might be.

"Simon, I think… I think whoever posted this is dangerous." I sink back into the rolling chair, biting down on my lip to keep it from trembling. Simon hops up on the computer desk, his brows pulled together in deep contemplation.

"What do you mean they're dangerous?"

"Think about it," I tell him. "Neither one of us remembers there being anyone else in the woods that night. We were out there for, what? A half hour after that thing killed Renée, maybe longer? Then we walked home. Through the woods. Together. And that whole time, it was just us."

"Yeah, so what?"

"*So,*" I shoot back, failing to disguise the exasperation in my voice, "if we were the only ones out there, but this reelbigfoot19 person also claims to have been there and they also know details about Carissa's death—details that only a person who was there could know—then don't you think that's a little too... coincidental?"

"Wait, are you saying what I think you're saying?" Simon's eyes are so wide, they look like two chocolate coins about to pop out of his skull. Because even though I don't say it out loud, he knows exactly what it is I'm saying. There's only one way that three people could have witnessed what happened to Renée that night. Two of them were hiding in the forest, trying not to be seen. The other was standing over her, watching the life drain from her body.

There is a monster in Whitehall. Just not the one we thought.

Chapter 14

Simon and I sprint from the back office and make a beeline for the front door of the Bigfoot Museum.

"Be back soon, Mom! Promise," Simon hollers over his shoulder, not waiting to hear Mrs. Little's response as we push through the glass door, the Sasquatch call howling out behind us as we flee from the building and pile into Mom's Beetle. Heavy raindrops pelt the roof of the car as I try to get it started. The engine stutters to life on the second attempt and I pull out of the parking lot, navigating through the dampened streets until we inevitably arrive outside my house. I kill the ignition once we're parked in the driveway, and together we race through the rain, up the creaky wooden steps of my front porch, spilling in through the door in a flurry as I unlock the deadbolt.

Dad and Riley are still at the general store, so it doesn't worry me that the house is dark and quiet when we enter. In fact, I prefer it this way. It makes what I have to do next that much easier to accomplish.

Simon and I climb the staircase to the second floor and make our way to my room. He plops down on the window seat, bringing one of his long legs to his chest while the other dangles over the edge of the seat in front of the built-in bookcase beneath.

"So, let me get this straight," he says as I sling my backpack around the back of my desk chair. "You think there's some sort of serial killer out there impersonating Sasquatch?"

"I mean, when you say it out loud, it sounds kind of nuts," I confess. "But yeah. That's the gist of it."

"And you think they're using a ghillie suit to pull it off?" It's a question, but the way Simon says it makes me feel like he thinks I've gone completely off the deep end. My cheeks burn with righteous indignation as I fix him with a scathing stare.

"How is that any harder to believe than an *actual* bigfoot being out in the woods?" Simon sucks on his teeth and shrugs.

"Touché." He slides his other leg over the edge of the window seat and leans his back against the glass pane behind him. "Okay, so if you think it's an imposter, why are we here? Why aren't we talking to the police?"

I pinch the bridge of my nose and shut my eyes, unable to shield my aggravation from the sheer stupidity of his questions. Are all boys this dumb?

"I *can't* go to the police," I remind him. "If I do, they're just gonna ask me why I was out in the woods the night Renée died. And once they get it out of me that I'm the one who helped slash her tires—and you *know* they will—then nothing I say is gonna matter to them. No. I'm not going to the police. Not yet, anyway. We need to find out who it is first. Come to them with real proof."

"Okay... how are we gonna do *that?*" The corners of my mouth twist into my cheeks as I give Simon a sly grin. I've already thought this through.

"Wait here," I instruct him. "I'll be right back."

Before he can respond, I leave Simon sitting on the window seat and head down the hallway, past the bathroom, into my dad's room at the end of the corridor. The master bedroom is only a few feet bigger than mine in either direction, with the same half-paneled walls and scratched hardwood floors. I step past the king-sized bed in the center of the room beneath the set of double-hung windows on the wall furthest from the door and over to the walk-in closet. A twinge of guilt surges through me for poking around in my dad's stuff but it only lasts a moment. This is important. I know he'd understand. You know… if I told him. Which I'm not going to. Not until I know I'm right and I find out whoever's doing this.

My eyes land on a big, plastic box hiding in the corner of the closet that I instantly recognize when I see it. *Jackpot.* I hustle over to the spot where it's resting on the floor and bend down to scoop it into my arms. It's one of those file organizer boxes—the kind people use to keep important documents—so it's kind of awkward to hold and it weighs a ton from all the piles of paper that I know are tucked inside. Lifting with my legs, I manage to hoist it up, only groaning a little when I stand to full height and stagger out of the closet, past my dad's bed, down the hall, and into my room. Simon sees me struggling with the box and jumps to his feet.

"Geez, E, let me help you with that." He rushes to my side and takes the box from my hands. Even though he's skinny and his arms look weak, he makes it look easy as he lifts the container from my arms and carries it across the room, placing it carefully at the foot of my bed. "Dang, that's heavy. What the heck's in that thing anyway?"

I join Simon by the foot of my bed and take a seat on the edge of the mattress, leaning over to pop the top off the file box and reveal the sea of papers stacked in neat little rows inside.

"It's my dad's old file box," I explain. "He keeps hard copies of all the sales he's made at the store. Says it helps him know what people want. Kind of like when we do inventory, but this is a little more detailed because it's got a record of everything. Even things we don't carry anymore."

Simon lets out a low whistle and raises his eyebrows.

"Impressive," he comments. "But why doesn't he just keep all this on the computer?"

I roll my eyes and pause my rifling fingertips as they parse through the tightly packed folders inside the box.

"You know my dad," I say. "He *hates* technology. Wouldn't even let me get an iPhone until I saved up enough money from what he pays me at the shop to get one. I'm sure he's got a digital file of all this somewhere on that ancient computer of his, but for the most part, it's all in this box."

"That seems hard to believe." Simon takes a seat next to me on the bed, watching as I fumble through each file, occasionally stopping to pull one out and see what's written on the label before deciding it's not the one I'm looking for. "Hasn't your dad owned that store for, like, twenty years or something? How is it possible that all his records fit in one box?"

"Oh, they don't," I agree. "He's got a whole bunch of them in a storage container out by Fort Anne. But this is everything for 2023 so far."

"Okay, so what exactly are you looking for?"

As the question leaves his lips, I extract a manilla folder with the words "Hunting Gear" written on the label. *Eureka!* I turn to Simon and wave the file in his face, a triumphant smile tugging at my lips.

"This is what I'm looking for," I tell him. "This is the record of everyone who's bought a ghillie suit from our store since the start of the year."

A flash of understanding flickers across Simon's face and he grins. As the reigning champion of the Bigfoot Festival's annual costume contest, he knows better than anyone how convincing my dad's ghillie suit selection is for those looking to pass as a sasquatch. If the person on the message board is a local, there's a good chance their name is on the list of customers who have made a purchase.

I thumb the folder open and pull out the stack of papers contained within. My heart sinks.

"Oh no," I groan.

"What's the matter?" Simon leans in so his head is practically resting on my shoulder, straining to get a better look at the list in my hands.

"Look at all these names!" I smack the paper with the back of my hand. "Mr. Gosselin, Mr. Truman, Mr. Atkins, Mrs. Feldman, Ms. Thomas—*you*. Just about everybody in town is on this list. There's no way we'll find out who it is just from this. I don't know what I was thinking."

Simon snatches the paper out of my hands as I flop back on the bed and cover my face in my hands, letting out a frustrated grunt.

"I don't mean to burst your bubble even more or anything, but..." He hesitates like he's afraid to hear my reaction to what he's about to say and I let out another animalistic groan of aggravation.

"Just say it," I tell him.

"Well, it just hit me: We're only looking at the suits that were bought *this* year," he says. "But that post was from *four* years ago. We'd need to look at the list from 2019. And that's only assuming the person bought the suit from your dad's store. They could've gotten it from anywhere that sells hunting gear. Heck, they could've gotten it way before 2019 and just decided to use it for... well, you know."

Crap.

He's right. I don't know why I thought that stupid list was going to have all the answers. What do I think I am—some sort of detective? I'm just a kid. A stupid, naïve, irrational idiot who can't even—

"Woah, wait a minute." Simon interrupts my negative self-talk and lays back on the mattress so our shoulders are touching as he shoves the list back in my face. "Did you know Asher Pope is on this list, too?"

My pulse quickens at the sound of Asher's name. I pluck the paper out of Simon's hands and hold it out so I can read it. Sure enough, I see the words "Asher Pope" staring back at me in my dad's slanted chicken scratch.

"Check out the date." Simon lifts his eyebrows when I turn my head to face him as though using them to point back to the paper in my hands. I take another look at the date written beside Asher's name and my breath catches in my throat.

"Oh my God," I gasp. "That was last week! Just two days before Carissa was killed."

A heavy silence falls over us as we let the discovery settle. I know it's not convincing enough to take to the police, but I can't help feeling like this is significant. Of all the people on that list, Asher is the only person with a direct connection to Renée's death. I don't have any siblings, but I've seen the way Carissa and Kate used to interact with theirs. The twins were always stampeding into Kate's room unannounced, only to get chased out by their fuming older sister while she hurled threats into their backs as they fled the scene. Carissa's older sister, Christina, never had a kind word to say, her constant criticisms probably one of the reasons why Carissa was so keen to mock others. Maybe Asher and Renée had a sibling rivalry of their own. Maybe he got tired of it until he finally snapped. Maybe after he killed her, he realized that he liked it, and he wanted to do it again.

"What're you thinking?" Simon pulls me out of my private musings and I twist to face him, digging my elbow into the bed as I prop my head up in the palm of my hand. He mirrors my posture so we're each lying on our sides, facing one another. For the first time since entering the house, it dawns on me that we're alone.

Together.

In my room.

On my bed.

The butterflies are flapping around so wildly in my stomach that I feel like one might float out of my mouth. But I can't keep quiet for too long or I'll look like even more of a weirdo.

"I don't know what to think," I admit. "What about you? What're you thinking?"

His eyes slide from my face until they land on something I can't see and the corners of his lips quirk upward.

"I *think* you've got fuzz in your hair." He reaches over to pluck a dust bunny out of my tresses that must have landed in my hair while I was rummaging through Dad's closet. As he pulls his hand away, he tucks a loose lock behind my ear and I feel like I'm going to throw up from how hard my heart is racing. The way his eyes go all sleepy when he looks at me, I can tell he wants to kiss me. And I don't know... maybe I want that, too? Then again, maybe I don't. Simon is my best friend and things are already so weird right now with everything else going on. Do I really need to complicate my life even more by kissing my best friend? What if I'm terrible at it? What if it ruins everything? What if—

"E." Simon cuts through my thoughts yet again and when I snap back to reality, I realize that our noses are practically touching. His voice is just a murmur when he speaks again, "Can... can I—"

Before he can finish his thought, a bolt of electricity rattles down my spine as a loud buzzing noise bursts through the air. I spring from the bed when I realize the sound is coming from the bottom of my backpack as my phone vibrates angrily against the textbooks stored inside. Simon's eyes burn holes in the back of my neck as I reach my hand inside the bag to grab my cell, but I refuse to look at him. Not after what just happened.

"Oh *crap!*" I hiss when I pull the phone from my bag and tap the screen. I spin around to face Simon who is now leaning against the wall beside my bed with this sullen look on his face and his hands jammed in his pockets.

"It's my dad," I tell him, waving the phone in his direction like he can see all the missed calls displayed on the screen from his place across the room. "Oh, man. He's called me like, thirty times!"

Simon's expression turns from crabby to concerned in an instant.

"Did he leave a message?" I check the screen to find an answer to Simon's question and find that there are five voicemails waiting for me. I enter my passcode and bring the phone to my ear to listen to the most recent message.

"Eliza." There's panic in my dad's voice when he says my full name—the name he *never* uses unless he's mad or disappointed or scared. I try not to think about the last time he said my name like that. How it changed everything. I'm so focused on the tone of his voice and what it might mean that I don't even pay attention to the other words that come through the phone. I rewind the message and play it over from the beginning, this time hanging on every word.

"Eliza, it's your father. Come down to the store as soon as you get this message. It's an emergency. Hurry."

Chapter 15

Of course, the rain is coming down so hard when I climb into the Beetle that I can hardly see through the windshield. There's no time for me to drive Simon back to the museum, so he calls his mom to pick him up while he waits on my front porch. I feel bad leaving him there—especially after what just happened between us—but all I can think about right now is getting to Dad. Thankfully, the car doesn't give me any trouble starting up, so I'm out of the driveway and on the road in no time. I'm driving so erratically that I nearly hydroplane into the gas station by the corner of the bridge that spans the Champlain Canal. My mind is racing through all the possible scenarios that would have caused my dad to leave me that message.

It's an emergency.

I remember the last time he spoke those words to me. How he had picked me up from school, his hand gripping mine so tight as he ushered me through the hallways, his lips clamped shut to keep himself from screaming on the way to the hospital where Mom lay dying.

It's not like last time. It's not like last time. It's not like last time.

I repeat the words over and over as though they're magic and merely uttering them will be enough to change reality. But it isn't enough. Because when I get to the general store, there's a police car sitting in the parking lot and my heart drops to my knees. I feel the pressure build inside my sternum, rising to my throat until I feel like I'm going to suffocate from the panic. No amount of breathing exercises can help me calm my nerves as I unclip my seatbelt and race through the rain to the front entrance of Dad's shop.

"Dad?" My voice comes out as a half-scream over the sound of the bell chime as I push through the door. Riley wastes no time bellowing out a low howl when I enter. She pads along the hardwood to greet me by the door, but I don't pat her head like I normally would. There's no sign of Dad at the counter. There's no sign of anyone in the store period.

What is going on?

"Dad?!" The sound of my full-blown shriek sets Riley on edge and her barks punctuate my rising fear. I start pacing to the back of the shop to see if he's around the corner, but I don't make it past the snack aisle before the door beside the counter that leads to the back office opens.

"Honey?" Instant relief floods my senses at the sound of my dad's voice. I sprint to the doorway where he's standing and let the full weight of my body crash into him as I throw my arms around his torso and breathe him in, just to make sure it's really him. The faint scent of cleaning supplies and pine floats up my nose and tells me that I'm safe. He's safe. I'm not an orphan. But Dad's muscles are stiff around my body as he holds me to his chest, and I know something isn't right.

"Dad, what's going on? What happened? Why did you—"

"Is this your daughter, Mr. Loft?" An unfamiliar voice calls from behind Dad's shoulder and I freeze mid-sentence. I can tell before my eyes confirm it that the voice belongs to a woman, but the blunt edge of her words makes her sound more masculine. As soon as I peer past my dad's body, fresh dread swims through my veins when I find a uniformed police officer staring back at me. Dad clears his throat and places a protective hand on my shoulder before answering the officer's question.

"Yes, this is Eliza," he says. "Honey, this is—"

"Detective Barnes." The woman reaches out with a thin hand wrapped in translucent skin that I know she expects me to shake but I'm too scared to touch her. I'm afraid that if I do, she'll pull me in and slap cuffs around my wrists before I have time to wrench my hand away. She lets her hand hover in the air for a moment before realizing that I'm not going to return the gesture and letting it fall back to her side with a gentle thud. I twist around to face my dad.

"What's going on?"

His mouth falls open to speak, but once again the detective seizes the opportunity to interrupt him.

"I just stopped by the store to ask your father if it would be alright if I asked you a few questions." Detective Barnes reaches into her pocket and extracts a small notepad with one of those tiny pencils they give out at mini-golf courses shoved through the spiral wiring across the top. She flicks it open to an empty page and pries the pencil free before peeling her thin lips back into an even thinner smile that somehow looks like more of a frown.

"I–I don't understand," I stammer. "Am I in trouble or something?"

"That's what I'm here to find out," Detective Barnes replies, and I swear there's a gleam of satisfaction that dances across her dark blue eyes. Like she's *hoping* that she'll find a reason to haul me off to jail. I gulp.

"Sorry, but... what is this about exactly?" I turn from the detective to my dad and back again, bouncing between their faces in search of answers they seem reluctant to provide. Dad squeezes the spot where his hand is still clamped around my shoulder before dropping it to his side.

"Let me go lock up so we don't get disturbed and then we can talk more about... all this." He nods to the detective who seems pleased with the suggestion. Then he shuffles off to the front entrance, turning the sign hanging over the glass pane in the center of the door so that the, *Sorry, We're Not Open*, message is facing any would-be customers. I hear the lock click, followed by Dad's heavy footsteps as he walks back to where I'm still standing in the doorway to the back room, still no closer to understanding what the heck is going on than I was when I first got here. The panic and fear that I'd been feeling is now starting to make a full transformation to anger and frustration.

"Can someone *please* tell me what the heck is going on?" I fold my arms across my chest, darting my eyes back and forth between Dad and the detective once again. Detective Barnes steps out from the back office and walks around to the front of the counter while Dad takes his place behind the counter next to me, slinging a strong arm around my shoulders as he draws me closer to him.

"Before we get started, I just need your full name and address for the record," Detective Barnes states matter-of-factly, her tiny pencil poised above the notepad, ready to copy down my information.

"No," I protest.

"*Eliza*," Dad snaps, a warning tone in his voice. I crane my neck up at him and pout.

"I'm not saying anything until I know what this is about." Just as Dad's mouth falls open to reprimand me for what I'm sure he'll say is "rude" behavior, Detective Barnes interrupts him yet again. I'm getting really tired of this lady cutting him off so much.

"It's okay, Mr. Loft," she says, then turns her attention to me. "As I'm sure you know, a classmate of yours was killed last week. I'm here to follow up on some information I received regarding an incident that took place between the two of you prior to her death."

My eyes go so wide, they start to burn and tear. Detective Barnes pretends not to notice the effect her words have had on me, tapping her pencil on the empty page in her notebook with an almost bored look on her face. I quickly mutter my full name and address, which she jots down on the paper before tilting her head up to face me once more.

"That wasn't so hard, was it?" She smiles and the sight of it makes me nauseous with apprehension. "Okay, Eliza, let's start with the basics. How do you know Carissa King?"

My throat is dry and sticky like it wants to trap the words inside my lungs, but I fight through it.

"We went to school together," I answer. "She used to be my friend."

"Used to be?" One of Detective Barnes's dark brows arches over her eye. "Did you have a falling out or something?"

Crap.

I shouldn't have said that. Now I have no choice but to tell her the truth. I can't go back on what I said or she'll think I'm a liar.

"Um... yeah," I confess. "It was a long time ago, though."

"About how long ago was your fight?"

"Like, four years ago, I think." Detective Barnes scribbles down my response and peeks over at me once she's finished writing.

"What caused the fight?" My stomach flips when she asks the question and all I can see is the moonlight rippling across South Bay as Carissa, Kate, and I plunge my dad's hunting knife into the tires of Renée's little white sedan.

I must have drowned somewhere in the memory because Detective Barnes sounds annoyed when she presses me again.

"Eliza? What caused the—"

"It was just dumb drama," I blurt out. "I stood up for another kid in class who she didn't like. She got mad about it. That's all that happened."

My pulse is thrumming so hard against my jugular, I'm worried that the detective will see my neck throbbing and call me out for the half-truth but she doesn't. She just jots down more notes and peppers me with another question.

"Is that what your fight was about last Tuesday, too?" The color drains from my face and my knees feel like Jell-O.

How does she know about that?

The only people still alive who know that I fought with Carissa last week are Simon and Kate. I know Simon didn't go to the police about it, and I don't think it could have been Kate, either. But who else could it have been? It doesn't make sense.

"I... no. It wasn't about that this time," I tell the detective.

"What was it about, then?" My face feels hot and tingly. I don't want to lie, but I can't tell her the truth about why I was at the trailhead with Carissa and Kate that day.

Because if I tell her about those notes we got in our locker, she'll ask me what they said. And if I tell her what they said, she'll want to know what it meant. And if I tell her what it meant, that's it. I'm toast. So, I suck in a deep breath, and I say the first thing I can think of that even remotely resembles the truth.

"She was mad at me because of something that happened the day before," I explain, recounting the story about how I had watched Carissa making out with her boyfriend before math class. It's embarrassing and it makes me sound like a total jealous stalker freak, but that's better than getting locked up at seventeen for murdering my high school's cheer captain, isn't it? At first, I think it is, but Detective Barnes's next question tells me that she's far from writing me off as a suspect.

"So, it's safe to say that you're a little jealous of Carissa, then?" Her voice is smooth and even when she says it, but there's a darkness in her eyes that tells me I'm nowhere near her good side.

"It's understandable," she continues. "You two start off as friends, then you fight. She gets to be the pretty, popular one while you get tossed to the side. Now she's dating the guy you like. Things like that can get messy fast."

Cold sweat trails down the nape of my neck as I realize what it is she's insinuating. She thinks I had it out for Carissa. She thinks our fight is what led to her death.

She thinks I did this.

Oh my God. This is it. My life is over. I'm going to jail. Any second now, she's going to walk around the counter, place the handcuffs around my wrists, and—

"What exactly are you accusing my daughter of, detective?" Dad's voice sounds scary when he speaks. I almost don't recognize it's him talking, but I can feel the vibration of his vocal cords rumbling through his chest like thunder. Detective Barnes straightens her back and snaps her notebook shut.

"I'm just making an observation, Mr. Loft, that's all."

"Well, unless you have a subpoena ready, I think we've heard enough of your *observations* for one day," Dad seethes. "Now, if you don't mind, I have a business to run."

The tension between Dad and Detective Barnes as they stare each other down across the countertop is so palpable, for a moment I think lasers might shoot out of their eyes or something. With a tap of her knuckles against the counter, Detective Barnes tucks the notepad back inside her pocket and starts to make her way toward the front entrance. Before she reaches out to unlock the door, she spins around to face the counter once again.

"Just one more question before I go and then I'll leave you to it." Her blue eyes land on me and I swallow hard around the lump of fear that's lodged in my throat as I anticipate what it is she's going to ask. "Is there anyone who can account for your whereabouts on Tuesday evening between the hours of four o'clock and ten o'clock?"

A wave of relief washes over me when I realize that there is someone who can vouch for me. Two people, actually. Both of whom I trust more than anyone in the world to help clear my name of this mess.

"As soon as I left the trailhead, I went straight to Simon Little's house. I was there until around seven o'clock. Then he brought me back to my house. My dad came home from the shop maybe a half hour after that."

Detective Barnes nods her head and removes her notebook from her pocket. She asks me for Simon's contact information, which I give to her even though I don't want to. Once she's satisfied that she has everything she needs, she unlocks the door and walks out of the shop into the pouring rain.

Chapter 16

After the detective left, I stayed with Dad at the shop until closing time. I was too shaken up by the interrogation to go back to the empty house, and even though I desperately wanted to talk to him about it all, I was still feeling too embarrassed by what happened in my room earlier to go back to Simon's place. So, I settled for stocking shelves at the general store until eight o'clock rolled around and it was time to go home.

Dad and I haven't spoken two words to each other since it happened. It's starting to make me nervous. I was happy when he came to my defense earlier. At the time, I thought it meant that he believed I was innocent. But now I'm not so sure. When we got home from the shop, he just went straight to his room without even looking at me. He didn't even bother heating up a microwave meal for dinner. Not that I care. I'm not hungry anyway.

This whole thing sucks. First that note in my locker, then Carissa gets murdered by some psychopath pretending to be Bigfoot—who I'm still partially convinced is Asher, by the way—and now the police think *I'm* the one responsible? None of it makes any sense. I mean, if what Simon and I read in that post is true and Carissa really was torn apart like that, how could the police possibly think I did it? Soaking wet, I weigh about a hundred and ten pounds, but I somehow ripped the arms and legs off one of my classmates and stuck her torso in a bush?

Part of me thinks it's ridiculous, but then I remember what I said to Simon about those girls in Wisconsin. They stabbed their friend nineteen times through the heart and left her for dead in the woods. If they could do all that at twelve years old, maybe it's not a stretch to think that I could have hurt Carissa. Except it is a stretch, because it's not true. I'm innocent. And once again, no one believes anything I say. I'm so tired of always being ignored. I'm so tired of being alone. I just want all of this to go away. But most of all, I just want my mom. I miss her like crazy, and I know if she were here, she'd know exactly what to say. She always did.

I roll over in bed and shove my face into my pillow as I let the tears come. At first, the sobs are soft and quiet as they're deafened by the fabric of my pillowcase. But the more I let them free, the louder they become until my heartache fills the entire room so I don't even hear Dad's footsteps when they travel down the hallway into my bedroom. The depression on the bed as he sinks into the mattress next to me and places his hand on my back is what alerts me to his presence.

"E, honey?" He rubs the space between my shoulder blades, but I don't face him. I just continue crying into my pillow, wishing this all would end.

"C'mon, sweetheart," Dad tries again. "I want to talk to you. Please look at me."

I try my best to calm down, sucking in a few deep breaths before pressing into my palms and rising to a seated position beside my dad on the bed. He places his arm around my shoulders and I lean into him, tears still gliding silently down my cheeks before they fall onto my lap.

"Did Mom ever tell you why she stopped talking to Gramma?" The question catches me so off guard when it leaves my dad's lips that it puts a stop to my crying altogether. I tilt my head up at him and bunch my brows together in a knot.

"No, she didn't." Dad breathes out a heavy sigh in response.

"I figured that," he says. "You weren't old enough to understand back then. Still aren't, if I'm being honest. But it's time you know."

He looks across the room at the same window seat where Simon was sitting just a few hours earlier. There's a heaviness in Dad's eyes that feels all too familiar. He carried the same weight in his stare all through Mom's funeral. Whatever it is that he's about to tell me, I already know it's not going to be good.

"You remember Grampa Jay?" My lips curl back into a smile despite the grim expression on Dad's face.

"Of course, I remember him." I giggle as memories of my grandpa's whacky faces and slapstick humor fill my head. "He was always so funny. I miss him sometimes."

Dad stiffens at the comment and I watch his jaw muscles flex as he grinds his teeth down on words he wants to say but doesn't. He clears his throat and relaxes a bit.

"Yeah, well, sometimes people can look one way on the outside but be another way on the inside," he says.

"What do you mean?"

"I mean that what happened between Mom and Gramma wasn't Gramma's fault. Not completely. She just couldn't handle it, I guess." His throat bobbles as he swallows, his eyes still trained on the window seat, refusing to look at me.

"Handle what?" As soon as I ask the question, Dad brings his free hand to his face and covers his eyes just long enough to squeeze out a few tears into his fingertips. He takes a quivering breath and lowers his hand back to the bed before answering me.

"Your grandfather did some terrible things to your mom when she was young." His words land like an anvil in my stomach and even though I don't want to know the answer, I ask the question anyway.

"What do you mean? What kinds of things?" Dad presses his lips together in a tight line and I'm reminded once again of that day he came to pick me up from school. Except he doesn't look scared the way he did back then. He looks angry. And... haunted.

"Sometimes... sometimes adults do things—*bad* things—because they know they can. Because they know that no one will believe the people they've hurt."

"But what did he—"

"What he did to your mom isn't worth repeating," Dad says sharply and the force of his words is enough to snap my mouth shut. His eyes soften as they land on mine and he gives my shoulder a gentle squeeze.

"I'm sorry, honey," he mutters as he kisses the top of my head. "It's just... some things are too painful to relive. And what he did caused your mom a lot of pain. She didn't want to talk about it with anyone because she was afraid that no one would believe her. And when she finally did tell someone about it, her worst fears came true."

A flicker of understanding flashes through my mind before the words leave my lips to confirm it.

"She told Gramma?" Dad gives a solemn nod and my heart feels like it's going to burst. I don't know what Grampa did to my mom, but I have a pretty good idea. And the fact that her own mother wouldn't listen to her makes me so angry and heartbroken that I just want to scream. My mind is spinning so fast and even though I know it's not fair, I'm a little annoyed with my dad for dumping all of this on me. Doesn't he see that I have enough on my plate as it is? The words tumble out of my mouth before I can stuff them back in.

"Why are you telling me this?"

That's when Dad pulls away, but only so he can place a hand on each of my shoulders and look me straight in the eyes when he speaks next.

"I'm telling you this because what happened between Mom and Gramma wasn't right," he says. "A parent needs to be there for their child, no matter what. Gramma and

Grampa weren't there for your mom like they should have been, and I saw how it affected her. I never, ever want you to feel that way, honey. I never want you to feel like you can't talk to me. I am always, *always* here for you. Even if it's scary, even if it's embarrassing, even if you think it'll get you into trouble, you can always come talk to me."

He pulls me into his arms and smooths my hair as we embrace. I bury my face in his chest as fresh tears sting at the back of my eyes, but I don't let them come this time. Because even though my dad just finished telling me that I can talk to him about anything and part of me wants to believe him, an even bigger part of me knows that I can't. And the moment he sees me crying, he's going to know that I'm hiding something. As if he can hear the thoughts swirling around inside my head, he pulls away and holds me at arm's length as he peers inside my soul.

"Is there anything you want to talk about, sweetheart?" he asks me.

I want to say yes. I want to tell him all about the slashed tires. I want to tell him all about what I saw in the woods. I want to tell him all about the note in my locker. I want to tell him *everything*.

But I don't.

"I just really miss Mom," I tell him, and the instant I say it, I feel guilty. Because even though it's the truth, somehow it's still a lie.

Chapter 17

Mom's Beetle starts up just fine this morning, which only strengthens my theory that the car has a mind of its own and it's actively plotting against me. If it wasn't, then it would know that school is the last place on earth that I want to be and it would do everything in its power to keep me from getting there. Instead, the engine comes to life right away, placing me in the Whitehall High parking lot with twenty minutes to spare until homeroom. Plenty of time for me to run into Simon for yet another awkward encounter. *Perfect.*

He's leaning against my locker when I round the corner and as soon as I see him, I stop dead in my tracks. All I can think about is the last time we were together. How he pulled that piece of fuzz out of my hair. How the tip of his nose was so close to mine. How he looked at me. When did everything get so complicated between us? Why can't I just have my friend back? Will things ever just go back to normal?

Simon peels his back off my locker and straightens himself as I approach, his eyes swimming with a curious combination of worry and fear when his gaze lands on me.

Oh no.

"Hey, is everything okay?" he mutters in a low voice. I have no idea how to even begin to answer that question, so I don't. Instead, I sidestep him and enter my locker combination, doing my best to ignore the feel of his eyes as they linger on the back of my neck, prickling my skin. Maybe if I refuse to answer, this will all go away and he'll drop it. But he doesn't. He just moves to the locker next to mine and leans against it, watching me intently as I trade the books in my backpack for the ones I need for my first few classes of the day.

"E." He places his hand on mine, stopping me from grabbing the next textbook and forcing me to look at him. "Please talk to me. I know something happened last night."

I yank my hand away and snatch the last book out of my locker, dropping it in my bag and slamming the metal door shut with enough force that the sound makes Simon jump back. Well, either that or it's the look on my face when I turn to him that forces him to cower away in fear.

"*Nothing* happened last night," I hiss. I know it's wrong and I know it's unfair to be so callous towards him, but I don't want to talk about this. Not here. Not now. Not ever. But Simon won't take no for an answer.

I push past him and start walking toward Mrs. Morton's classroom even though I don't need to be there for another ten minutes. Instead of dropping the subject like I want him to, Simon jogs to catch up with me down the hall so he can keep pestering me with questions I don't want to answer.

"You're lying," he insists. When I don't stop walking, he grabs me by the wrist which forces me to spin around and look at him. As my mouth drops open to give him a piece of my mind, he beats me to the punch. He leans in close and in a low voice, he tells me, "A detective came to my house last night asking about you. Wanna tell me what the heck that's all about, or are you gonna keep pretending like nothing happened?"

My heart stutters before it stops beating.

Crap.

With everything that happened between me and Dad last night, I forgot all about the fact that I gave Simon's information to Detective Barnes. I didn't think she'd go to him so quickly. My shoulders sag and I turn my gaze to the speckled linoleum at my feet. Guess I don't have a choice but to talk about it now. I owe my friend an explanation.

"I'm sorry." I sigh, tears already stinging at the back of my eyes. "That's why my dad called me so many times. A detective came to the shop yesterday wanting to ask me all these questions about..."

I trail off and bite my lip, unable to complete the thought. Like maybe if I don't say it out loud, it won't be true. But Simon doesn't let me test the theory for too long.

"About what?" he presses. I feel a tear roll down my cheek and I swipe it away before Simon can see it.

"She wanted to talk about Carissa," I finally admit. "The cops think... I guess they think I did it or something."

"They *what?*" Simon's lips keep opening and closing like a dying fish gasping for water that won't reach his gills. "H–how can they think that?" he finally stammers. "I mean, you know what happened to her. There's no way you could have—"

"I know," I interrupt before he can remind me of the horrific details surrounding Carissa's death. "But that's the way it looks right now. They think I'm, like, super jealous of her or something. Like maybe I... y'know... because she was bullying me or whatever and I got tired of it or something."

"That's crazy," Simon argues.

"Is it?" I challenge him. "Doesn't sound that crazy to me. Especially not considering the fact that I'm one of the last people to have seen her alive. And we were fighting at the time. Makes perfect sense why they'd think I did it. Heck, *I'd* think I did it if I were them."

"Yeah, but, E, you *didn't* do it," Simon reminds me. "You were with me for most of the night. There's no way you could have done that to her."

"I know." I hang my head and let the words fall to the floor. "That's why the detective came to your house last night. She asked me where I was between four o'clock and ten o'clock, so I told her I was with you."

I lift my head slightly as I dare to peek at Simon and gauge his reaction to my confession. He's rubbing the back of his neck and his eyebrows are scrunched together, but he doesn't look angry or annoyed. He just looks scared.

My stomach drops.

"What did you tell her?"

"I told her the truth," he insists. "I told her you showed up at my house around five, then I drove you back to the trailhead to get your car, and then you followed me back to your house."

All the blood in my body freezes at once and my vision blurs at the edges. I didn't mention anything to Detective

Barnes about going to get my car at the trailhead. It's not like I had anything to really hide about it, but I was afraid that if she knew I went back there during the times she specified, she would get even more suspicious of me. And of course, I didn't tell Simon anything about what I had told the investigator, so he wouldn't have known to cover for me.

Oh no. What have I done?

"What's wrong?" Simon sees the terror in my eyes and I can't avoid it. I have to tell him.

"I didn't tell the detective about leaving my car at the trailhead," I confess.

"You *what?*" Simon stops walking and throws his hands to the sky.

"I know, I know." I sigh. My gaze drops to the floor to keep from facing the dread and anguish radiating from my friend's eyes. "I just... I was afraid that if I told her, she'd think I went back there to hurt Carissa or something. I'm sorry, Si. It all happened so fast! I didn't know what to do!"

"Great," Simon mutters. "Just perfect. I try to do the right thing and tell the truth, and I just end up making everything worse."

"Hey, you don't know that."

"Yes, I *do* know that!" Simon raises his voice an octave as the fear overtakes him and a few students turn their heads in our direction. He takes a deep breath to regain his composure and continues in a low voice, "E, this is bad. If you say one thing and I say another, how do you think that's going to look in her eyes? Now she's gonna think you really are hiding something. Oh man... if this ends up getting you into major trouble, I don't think I'll ever forgive myself."

Simon throws himself against the nearest locker and hides his face in his hands. I sink my teeth into my bottom lip and shuffle over to him, grabbing him gently by the wrists to uncover his face before placing a hand on either shoulder and looking him directly in the eye.

"Nothing bad is going to happen to me, okay?" I say, and I can't tell if I'm trying to reassure him or myself. "And even if it did, I would never blame you for it."

In the blink of an eye, Simon closes the distance between us and wraps his arms around me, holding me to his chest as he buries his face in my neck. We've hugged each other plenty of times in the past, but this time feels different—and not just because I can feel him trembling with fear. He's not holding me like a buddy who he doesn't want to see hurt. He's holding me like Dad used to hold Mom before she went to get her cancer treatments. Like he wants to keep me in his arms forever so he never has to feel the emptiness of my absence. At first, I stiffen. Between the other students passing us in the hallway and the memory of what happened in my room yesterday, I can't help but feel awkward as he clutches me tighter to his torso. But the longer I stay in his embrace, the more comfortable it feels until finally, I stop fighting it and I feel my body relax against his, not wanting the moment to end.

"I'm sorry," he whispers, and the movement of his lips against my skin gives me goosebumps.

"It's okay," I murmur. "Everything is going to be okay."

Before either of us has time to contemplate whether or not there's any truth to what I've said, the bell to first period rings and we're forced to let each other go. *Awesome.* Now I'm late to Mrs. Morton's class.

Again.

It comes as no surprise when Mrs. Morton asks to speak with me after class, but that doesn't make her lecture on the importance of punctuality any less embarrassing. Or irritating. She lets me off with a sharp warning, but if I'm late again in the next month, I'll have a "first-class ticket to detention." Which is excellent. Because I don't have enough things to worry about at the moment. Like what the heck is going on between me and Simon. Or whether or not Detective Barnes is going to arrest me for lying to her. Or who told her about the fact that Carissa and I had a fight in the first place.

Instead of paying attention in any of my classes, I've been wracking my brain all morning trying to figure out that last point. I hate to admit it, but a small part of me did think it might have been Simon. After all, he's always the one suggesting that we talk to an adult. Maybe he thought it was the right thing to do. But the more I replay our conversation from this morning, the less convinced I become that he was the one who went to the police. He seemed genuinely shocked that an investigator showed up to speak with me at all. And given the fact that he proceeded to tell the detective all about bringing me back to the trailhead that night, he obviously doesn't have a problem telling the truth, the whole truth, and nothing but the truth. *So help me, God.* It couldn't have been him.

But if it wasn't him, then who was it?

I can think of only one other person who knows about what happened at Death Rock last week. One other person who was there to watch it all unfold. The more I think about it, the more it makes sense that Kate is the reason why the police are zeroing in on me. Maybe she thinks I got mad after she threatened me, so I went back to beat

Carissa to the punch. Maybe the reason Kate hasn't been in school is because she's afraid of what I might do to her. Maybe that's why Mrs. Richards said what she said to me yesterday.

Leave my daughter alone.

Oh my God. Is that what happened? Is that what she thinks of me? How many other people has Kate told? How many other people think I'm a monster?

Do I even want to know?

These are the thoughts that ricochet around in my head when I round the corner to Mr. Atkins's pre-calculus class and see Kate walking towards his open door from the opposite end of the hallway. Despite her best efforts to avoid my stare, our eyes lock. The moment they meet, a burst of adrenaline surges from deep within my abdomen, sending a fiery confidence coursing through my veins that propels me forward and forces me to confront her.

"Hey!" I holler, stopping her stride before she can reach the door. Her hazel eyes turn dark and stormy when they find mine and her posture goes rigid. I recognize that stance; I've seen her use it on Carissa a thousand times. She's ready for a fight, and I guess I'm feeling stupid enough to give it to her because I don't back down. I just keep walking at her until we're face-to-face, nothing but years of invisible bitterness and resentment separating us. I swallow hard around the panic swelling in my throat.

Here goes nothing.

"I need to talk to you."

Kate looks down the length of her nose at me, pursing her lips as she hugs the books in her arms tighter to her chest.

"I'm not supposed to talk to you," she grumbles. She tries to push past me, but I intercept her before she can bypass me and sneak into Mr. Atkins's room.

"Oh yeah?" I challenge her. "Did your mom tell you that, or did that advice come from Detective Barnes?"

Kate's smooth, caramel skin turns to ash at the remark and she tries to get past me once again, but I'm too quick. When she takes a step forward to the left, I jump out in front before she can squeeze past me. She takes a step to the right, and she has to pull her foot away to keep me from stomping down on it as I scurry to block her path.

"Get out of my way!" she snaps.

"No," I snap back. "Not until you tell me what the heck is going on."

"I don't know what you're talking about."

"Bull crap!" I hiss, leaning in as I lower my voice, "I know it was you who told the cops about what happened at Death Rock last week. Now they think I had something to do with what happened to Carissa!"

At the mention of Carissa, Kate's gaze sinks to the floor and she stops trying to get away from me. Instead, she plants her back into the nearest locker and chews on her bottom lip, refusing to meet my stare as she fights back the urge to cry. And even though I'm mad at her and I still don't forgive her for what happened at the trailhead or what she said to the cops or the years of hell she put me through alongside Carissa, I can't help but feel sorry for her. I fold my arms and lean against the locker beside her, so close that our shoulders touch and she doesn't flinch away.

"Why did you go to the cops?" I try again in a gentler voice. She heaves out a deep sigh and I pretend not to notice when she wipes a tear from her cheek.

"I didn't *go* to the cops," she explains. "*They* came to *me*. And I don't know why I told them. It's not like I was trying to get you in trouble or anything. I was just being honest about what happened. I've never been interrogated before. It was scary. I just... I just wanted to help them find out what happened to her..."

Kate's voice cracks and the rims of her eyes turn red as fresh tears flood to the surface. Part of me wants to put an arm around her shoulder and let her cry into my shirt like she did the day she got suspended for lashing out at Carissa. But I don't. Because even though I miss our friendship and even though I'm sad that she's hurting, I still can't forget all the times when she was the one responsible for reducing me to a puddle of tears as I sobbed against the closest locker.

And I still can't shake the feeling that she's lying to me.

"I don't get it," I tell her. "If you didn't tell the cops that you think I had something to do with it, why was your mom so rude to me when I came to your house yesterday?"

Kate presses her lips together so tight, the skin around them starts to turn white from the pressure. That combined with the fact that she still won't meet my eyes tells me that she's hiding something. It won't be long until the bell rings and we're both late for pre-calculus, but I won't let this go until I get an answer.

"I know you're not telling me everything. Just tell me what—"

"Okay, fine!" she blurts. "I... I told my mom."

"About...?"

"Are you really gonna make me say it?" Kate levels me with a look like she's trying to telepathically communicate with me. I don't hear whatever words she's silently shouting in my head, but I don't need to. I can see the image of our thirteen-year-old hands wrapped around the hilt of my dad's hunting knife reflected in her eyes.

My stomach turns to ice.

"Kate, you didn't."

"I had to!" she huffs, shaking her head as she grinds her teeth. "You don't know what it's like. My mom is... she's not like other moms, okay? She doesn't take 'no' for an answer, especially when it comes to her kids. And if I even *try* to hide *anything* from her, it's all, 'This is how you treat me after everything I do to come to this country?' I didn't have a choice. I had to come clean. Especially after we got those notes in our lockers? I was scared. What if that's why Carissa's dead? What if one of us is next?"

Her question hangs in the air like a dark cloud longing to unleash a torrential downpour. I've contemplated this since finding out Carissa was killed, but hearing Kate say it out loud somehow makes it scarier. Somehow makes the possibility more real. But then I remember those posts from the message board that Simon found, and a small, desperate part of me wonders whether we have this all wrong. Like maybe we aren't being targeted for what happened to Renée.

Maybe there's another reason why all of this is happening.

"Have you gotten any other messages since the first one?" Kate shakes her head when I ask the question, and I breathe out a sigh of relief. "Me either," I tell her. "Maybe that's a good thing? Like, maybe this isn't about... *you know what*."

Kate arches a thin eyebrow over her mascaraed lashes, wrinkling her forehead in confusion.

"What else would it be about?" As soon as the question leaves her lips, I give Kate a look that's equal parts exasperation and disbelief.

"C'mon, Kate. We both know Carissa wasn't the nicest person in the world." I nudge her arm with my elbow and the ghost of a smile flickers across her lips as she concedes the point. "Maybe what happened to her is just a coincidence. Maybe she got mixed up in something that she shouldn't have. You know she was always good at that."

Kate nods her head carefully like she's considering what I've said, but her eyes look far away as they glide past my shoulder and land on something in the distance. I turn around to glimpse what she's staring at, but all I see behind me are scattered students hurrying off to their classes and Mr. Atkins standing in front of the door to his room, ushering our classmates inside as they pass him. When I turn back around to face Kate, her gaze is fixed on the floor.

She's hiding something again, I can sense it.

"What's the matter?" I prod. "Do you know something?"

"Just forget about it," Kate mutters. "We have to get to class. There's a test today."

She straightens herself and attempts to walk toward Mr. Atkins, but I place my hand on her shoulder to stop her before she can get too far.

"I don't care about a stupid math test," I tell her. "Look, I know you hate me now and we haven't been friends for a long time, but we were close once, Kate. Really close. Doesn't that mean anything to you? Don't you think I deserve to know what's going on just as much as you do?"

Kate's shoulders sag and there's a strange expression in her eyes when she looks at me. Like there's a war going on inside her mind and she isn't sure which side is going to win: The one that sees me as nothing more than an outcast she can poke fun at, or the one that remembers once upon a time, we used to be best friends. I don't have to wait for very long to find out who the victor is. She lets out a frustrated sigh and mutters that same Jamaican curse word her mother used when I was at her front door yesterday.

"Look, I shouldn't be telling you this. So you've gotta promise that you won't say anything, okay?" She bites her lip and casts a nervous glance over her shoulder like she expects the FBI to drop down from the ceiling just for thinking what she's about to say too loudly. Once she's satisfied that the coast is clear, she leans in and tells me in a low whisper, "Carissa was having an affair."

My jaw unhinges so I can practically feel my chin scraping against the linoleum at my feet as I let out a gasp.

"*An affair?*" Kate slaps me on the shoulder with an open palm when the words leave my lips.

"Keep your voice down!" she hisses. "Yes. She was having an affair."

"With who? For how long?" The questions form in my mind faster than I have time to speak them, but I can tell Kate is done giving me answers from the way she seals her lips shut with an invisible zipper. But even if she did want to tell me everything, it doesn't matter anyway because Mr. Atkins is flagging us both down from his post outside his classroom.

"C'mon, ladies," he calls to us. "This test won't take itself. Get a move on!"

Kate scurries away before I can say another word and I reluctantly follow behind in her footsteps. Mr. Atkins might as well just give me an "F" now. There's no way I'll be able to pay attention to this test with Kate's words still echoing through my mind.

Chapter 18

Carissa wasn't always evil. Before she turned me into a social pariah, before that night in the woods, before we started acting out together, we were friends. Best friends. And after my mom died, our bond only got stronger.

We were both only twelve when it happened. The school year was just getting started. Kate was this shiny new person in our lives that we both instantly gravitated towards, drawn to her big city lights like moths to a flame. But the change that Kate's arrival brought was minor compared to the chaos that came with puberty. Our bodies were transforming, hormones running rampant, mood swings not nearly as fun as the swings we'd mount on the playground during recess back when we weren't too cool for such things. It was a pivotal time in my life, a time when I needed a mother more than anything in the world. Someone to help me navigate the waves of change that kept sweeping me farther away from the sandy, sunny shores of my childhood.

But death doesn't care about what you need. It comes without warning, takes everything from you until all you're left with are a bunch of broken pieces and no picture to guide you on how to fit them back together.

Carissa wasn't very good at puzzles, but she tried her best to be a good friend. To bind together the fractured parts of myself with the only glue she knew how to use: makeup, shopping, and boys.

"Oh em *gee*, E, you look hot!" she squealed as she finished applying a final coat of pink gloss on my lips. It was a Saturday afternoon, and I was sitting in the white, wooden chair that was normally tucked beneath the vanity in Carissa's oversized bedroom. The pink tufted seat cushion provided just enough comfort so my backside didn't go numb while I waited for her to put the finishing touches on my makeover. When she was satisfied with her work, she spun the chair around so that I faced the mirror.

"Ta-da!" she announced with pride. "Do you love it, or do you *love* it?"

I gazed into my reflection, trying to admire Carissa's handiwork while simultaneously swallowing down the urge to cry. It wasn't a bad makeup job that made my eyes burn with tears. With a high school senior as a sister and the mayor's prim and perfect wife as a mother, Carissa had more than her fair share of practice and guidance when it came to the art of getting dolled up. She had expertly applied the mascara to my lashes and blended the blush into my cheeks to give me a natural glow, bringing the look together with a simple pink glossy lip. My normally flat, straight hair had been transformed into an undulating sea of chestnut waves thanks to Carissa's curling iron prowess. I looked older. I looked beautiful.

I looked just like my mom.

"I love it." The lie made my throat constrict. I peeled my eyes away from the mirror before the tears could betray my dishonesty. Carissa clapped her hands together before throwing her arms around my neck and pulling me into a tight embrace.

"You really are so pretty, E," she whispered.

I never admitted as much to her face, but I had always been jealous of my best friend and her effortless good looks. Though we were the same age, her body was changing much faster than mine. I resented the way she already looked so grown-up with her full chest and budding curves, attracting attention from all the boys who I wanted so badly to impress but couldn't with my stick-figure frame and sullen attitude. She had it all, and I had nothing—not even a mom left to show me how I could possibly compete with all the Carissa Kings of the world. When she told me I looked pretty, it was the first time in weeks that I felt some semblance of happiness. Some sense of hope that I could figure this "being a woman" thing out after all.

"Okay," Carissa announced, releasing me from her embrace, "now that you're a certified hottie, it's time to put your new look to the test."

She waggled her brows at me with a mischievous glint twinkling in her eyes. Before I could ask her what she meant, her sister stormed into the bedroom, the look on her face full of thunder and lightning.

"What the *hell* do you think you're doing?" Christina demanded. She crossed the room without waiting for a response and snatched the pink makeup bag from off Carissa's vanity, shaking it in her face as she seethed. "Didn't I tell you to keep your dirty little hands off my stuff?"

"Oh what–*ever*!" Carissa rolled her eyes. "You're just jealous because no matter how much makeup you put on, it can't change the fact that you're ugly."

"What did you just say to me?" A fire raged in Christina's eyes as she glowered down at her sister.

"You heard me," Carissa taunted. "And you know it's true."

"Is not!"

"Is too! Why do you think all the guys in your grade can't take their eyes off me? They want the younger, hotter sister. Not...whatever this is." Carissa waved her hand around in front of her sister's face, alluding to the ugliness she claimed was there but which I couldn't see. Christina swatted Carissa out of the way and reached for her hair.

"You little bitch," she hissed as she yanked on a fistful of Carissa's blonde locks.

"Ouch! Mo–o–om!" Carissa grabbed hold of my hand and pulled me from the chair, dragging me behind her as we fled from the room in search of her mother. We descended the spiral staircase of their Victorian mansion and rounded the corner into the room that the Kings called the "front parlor" but that was two times the size of the living room in my house. Mrs. King was seated on the sofa by the bay windows with a magazine in one hand and a martini in the other. She looked regal with her platinum tresses pulled back into a French twist and a pearl necklace dripping down the front of her peplum blouse.

"What is it, dear?" she asked without lifting her eyes from the magazine.

"Christina pulled my hair and called me the 'b' word," Carissa blurted out. As soon as the words left her lips, Christina appeared at her side.

"Only after *she* stole my makeup bag—again!"

"Girls, please." Mrs. King took a generous sip from her martini before placing it down on a coaster on the marble side table beside her. "You're giving me a headache with all this bickering. Carissa, why don't you and Eliza go for a walk or something? Give your sister some space."

"Why do *we* have to go? Why can't *she* leave?" Carissa huffed. One icy glare from her mother was all it took for her to cave. "Fine," she grumbled. "Let's go, Eliza."

Once more, Carissa took my hand and forced me to follow her out of the room, through the front door, and onto the wraparound porch. As we descended the stone steps that led to her home, we ran into Kate.

"Hey, I was just coming to see if you wanted to hang out." She smiled.

"Totally!" Carissa flipped her hair over her shoulder and cast a frustrated glance at the house that we had left behind. "But we can't hang out here. My sister's being such a drama queen right now. Wanna go for a walk with us?"

"Sure." Kate fell in line beside me. The three of us walked through the short stretch of towering mansions that comprised Whitehall's wealthiest neighborhood until we reached the main village, trading the white picket fences and perfectly trimmed lawns for cracked sidewalks and warped siding on worn farmhouses. It wasn't a conscious decision to go to the soccer field beside the high school, but that's where we ended up—just in time to catch the end of Saturday's game.

We selected a spot in the metal bleachers that lined the edge of the field, blending in with the afternoon crowd of parents and siblings and classmates all there to support the team. I didn't know anything about soccer (I still don't), but I liked the way the older boys looked in their navy-blue uniforms as they raced to seize control of the ball. The makeover from Carissa must have given me some sort of confidence boost because I didn't even try to disguise the fact that I was staring. And when a sandy-haired player locked eyes with me from across the field, I didn't turn away. Not even when he smiled and winked in my direction.

Carissa noticed.

"*Oooh*, got a crush on lucky Number Thirteen, huh?" she teased, a malicious sparkle glimmering in her eyes that I struggled to place. If I didn't know any better, it almost looked like jealousy. "That's Asher," she informed me. "Total hottie. My sister's obsessed with him, but he won't give her the time of day. It's hilarious. You should talk to him after the game!"

I blushed and forced my eyes away from the field. Looking was one thing, but talking? To a boy? A boy much older than me at that? No. It didn't matter how much makeup I had on or how good my hair looked. There was no way I could summon enough confidence to attempt a full-blown conversation with a high school senior. Hard pass.

"I don't know, Carissa," I mumbled. "I don't think I'm ready for all that. He's so much older than us. He doesn't want anything to do with me."

Carissa tossed her head back and opened her mouth wide, letting the wind carry her high-pitched cackle through the cheering crowd. She wiped a nonexistent tear from her eye and fixed me with a look that was saturated in equal parts condescension and derision.

"Oh, E, you're so cute." She patted me on the head like a toddler. I gripped the edge of the bleachers to keep myself from smacking her hand away like Christina had in her bedroom. "Don't you know that's what all older boys want? But hey, if you're too scared, that's fine. Just means there's more for me."

Her lips peeled back into a sinister grin while I pressed mine together to keep from shouting something I might regret. If she noticed my irritation, she didn't acknowledge it. Instead, she shot up from her seat, whooping and hollering at the field with all the enthusiasm of a proud girlfriend rooting on her man.

"Yeah, go Asher! C'mon baby, you can do it! WOOOO!"

Just as Asher scored the final point for his team, he spun around to face the bleachers and caught sight of his personal cheerleader waving and wiggling her fingers in his direction like the provocative little princess she was. She brought her fingers to her lips and blew a kiss into the air. My stomach twisted when he reached out to grab it and placed the invisible treasure in his pocket.

"See?" Carissa said with a satisfied smirk. "I know what they want. They're all the same."

Chapter 19

I don't have a single clue what was on that math test. From the moment Mr. Atkins placed the exam sheet down on my desk to the instant the bell rang signaling the end of pre-calculus, all I could think about was what Kate told me about Carissa.

She was having an affair.

Several thoughts vie for center stage as they race around my mind like a broken carousel. I'm ashamed to admit that the first thought I have is of Joel Baker and whether or not he knew his girlfriend was cheating on him (and what his reaction would be if someone were to break the news to him). Maybe if he knew what she was really up to, he'd be less sad about her being gone and more willing to move on. Perhaps with a totally different kind of girl. Like one who wears ripped jeans and rock band tees and has pink streaks in her hair.

Stop it, Eliza. Focus!

The next thoughts I have are all centered on finding the answer to one question: Who was Carissa having an affair with? It doesn't shock me to know that she was cheating on her boyfriend. Even when we were far too young to be thinking about boys in that way, Carissa was always a bit promiscuous. That day at the soccer field was just one of many occasions when her flirtatiousness couldn't be contained. But if Carissa was messing around behind Joel's back with another guy from school, wouldn't Kate have just called it cheating? Instead, she used the word "affair."

I know it technically means the same thing, but I just have this sinking feeling that it means more than that. I mean, isn't "affair" the word you use when one of the people cheating is married? Despite how my nightmares sometimes liked to torment me with visions of their wedding, Carissa and Joel weren't married. But maybe whoever Carissa was having the affair with was. Or maybe neither of them was married. Maybe Kate used that word because on some level, it gives her the same impression that it gave me when I heard her say it.

Carissa was involved with someone older than us. Much older.

I'm so focused on trying to figure out who the mystery man was in Carissa's life that I almost faint when I see Mr. Pope welcoming students into his room as I make my way to English class. It's not until my gaze lands on his broad shoulders and brooding eyes that I remember everything Simon and I discovered before my dad called me to come to the store. Those posts on the message board. The ghillie suit angle. Asher Pope's name on my dad's list. I know it's not enough to go on—tons of people in town have purchased hunting gear from our shop over the years—but I still can't keep the goosebumps from rising on my arms and neck as I skirt past Mr. Pope and file into the classroom without making eye contact.

"Hey." Simon greets me with an anxious smile when I take my seat. "You doing alright?"

"I... I don't know," I confess. The response makes him grimace.

"I really am sorry, E. You know I would take it back if I could in a—"

"No, no, I'm not upset about that. Honest," I assure him. "I just... something happened."

"Oh?" Simon twists in his seat so his body faces mine head-on. He props his elbows up on his desk and cradles his head in his hands, staring at me with expectant eyes the same way Riley looks at me when she's begging for a tasty treat. "Out with it already. Don't keep a guy waiting!"

I roll my eyes and smirk despite myself. Even when all I want to do is scream and cry, Simon always knows how to put a smile on my face. I love him for that. As a friend. I think...

"I ran into Kate just now." Simon jerks his head back like he can't believe what I'm saying.

"She's back?" I nod and he doesn't even let me draw a breath to explain before he's hammering me with more questions. "So, how did it go? What did she say? Did you find anything out?"

"Geez, slow down, would ya?" I tease. He rolls his eyes and points to the ticking clock hanging above the open classroom door.

"You'd better spit it out before the bell rings."

"Alright, alright." I put up my hands in defense. "Basically, she was the one who told the cops about me being at the trailhead last week."

Simon's lids stretch wide around his eyes.

"She *what?*" I can see the vengeance coursing through his veins as Simon's face dots pink with anger. "Why the hell would she do that? I mean really, what the f—"

"*Simon*," I cut him off before he can curse. "She didn't do it to get me in trouble. It just sort of... happened. She was just scared and thought she was doing the right thing by telling the truth. Can't you understand what that's like?"

The redness in Simon's cheeks deepens as he sinks back in his chair and folds his arms across his chest.

"Whatever," he grumbles.

"*Anyway*," I continue, choosing to ignore his sullen expression. "I also found out the reason why her mom was so rude to me yesterday." I lean in closer so my body is hanging over the side of my desk and whisper, "She told her mom about the tires."

That seems to snap Simon out of his funk. He straightens in his seat at once and turns to face me, his eyes like two balloons ready to burst from their sockets.

"No way," he gasps. "So, what's gonna happen now?"

"Honestly, I don't know." I lean back in my chair and bring my thumb to my teeth, nibbling at my nail the way I know Mom would hate if she were around to see me do it. Simon appraises me with an incredulous stare.

"You don't seem as worried about it as I thought you would be," he observes. "There's something else isn't there?"

Before I can open my mouth to answer Simon's question, Mr. Pope closes the door with a loud crack and takes his place in front of the whiteboard. I mouth the word "later" to Simon and he situates himself in his seat so he's facing the front of the room, waiting to hear our teacher's instructions like the rest of the class.

"Good afternoon, class," Mr. Pope addresses the room and the sound of his voice sends shivers down my spine. "Before we get started on today's reading, I'd like to pass out the results from your recent homework assignments. As you know, this was the first assignment given under my instruction, so you may notice a difference in the way I grade versus how Mrs. Sneider did things. If you have any questions or concerns, don't hesitate to come to me after class to discuss further."

I groan inwardly at his warning. I'm not usually a bad student. Sure, I show up late to Mrs. Morton's class occasionally and okay, maybe I don't have a full grasp of the French language like a third-level student should, but I'm proud of my B+ average. I worked hard for it. But with everything that's been going on since the start of senior year, I feel like all that hard work is starting to slip away. If I'm not careful, I might not have good enough grades to even make it into college. And I have a bad feeling that the homework results that I'm about to receive are only going to amplify those fears even more.

Mr. Pope pulls open the top drawer of what used to be Mrs. Sneider's desk and extracts a sheaf of papers from within. He waltzes to the opposite end of the room and, with agonizing deliberation, begins passing out each graded assignment to its corresponding student. I'm seated in the second row from the wall furthest from the classroom door, so I have to wait for Mr. Pope to get through a full three rows of students before he finally gets to me. When he arrives in front of my desk, I feel my cheeks turn bright pink as our eyes lock. It only happens for a fraction of a second, but it's long enough for me to feel like I'm suffocating in the cold, barren wasteland that blankets his stare. He licks the tip of his finger and pries one of the pages free from the pile in his hands.

"Good work," he mutters as he places the assignment down on my desk. At first, I'm relieved when I see a big, red "A" staring back at me. But then I see what's written in the margins and all the blood feels like it's draining from my body:

I know you did a lot of close reading for this. Well done!

The message itself isn't concerning. If anything, it's encouraging. I did a good job. I should be happy. But I am completely and totally the opposite of happy. Because the more I read what's written in front of me, the stronger the feeling of déjà vu becomes. This might be the first graded assignment that Mr. Pope has handed back to us, but there's no doubt in my mind that I've seen his handwriting before.

And I'm not the only one.

Chapter 20

"Are you sure it's a match?" Simon is grasping at straws trying to come up with reasons why I shouldn't be panicking, but he's not doing a good enough job at shielding the terror on his face as he cranes his neck over the cafeteria table and absorbs the side-by-side handwriting samples I have splayed across its surface. He knows just as well as I do that they're identical.

"I'm positive." I push the papers closer to him so he can get a better look. "He even uses some of the same words, see? 'I know,' 'you,' 'did.' And look at the writing itself. See how the letters are in all capitals, and how he connects the 'o' and 'u' together like he's switching to cursive halfway through? It's him, Si. Mr. Pope is the one who put the note in my locker."

Simon stares for a moment at the pages on the table before dragging his hands through his shaggy, dark hair and removing the glasses from his face. Like maybe if he can't see the evidence staring him in the eyes, it will somehow make it less true. He pinches the bridge of his nose and bunches his brows together.

"I don't get it," he gripes. "Why would a teacher threaten a student like this? It doesn't make sense!"

"I mean, it kind of does, doesn't it?" Simon looks up at me, the fierceness in his eyes wordlessly demanding an explanation for my comment as he places his glasses back on his face. "Think about it," I tell him. "If Asher knows we were out in the woods that night while he was busy murdering his sister and he thinks we know something or saw something we shouldn't, it would make perfect sense why he'd want to try and scare us. Or hurt us."

My words hover in the air like thick fog creeping over the Champlain Canal after a heavy rain. As though under a shared spell, Simon and I turn towards the empty seat at the end of the table where all the popular kids are busy scarfing down their lunches. The seat that used to be Carissa's before Asher decided to end her life.

Kate is sitting in the seat across from the one that once belonged to her best friend and I notice how she tries hard not to look at it. Instead, she keeps her attention tuned on

Brittany Wheeler, who doesn't seem to register the pain in her audience's eyes that I can see clear as day from all the way across the room.

"I'll be right back," I mutter to Simon. He doesn't have time to protest before I'm halfway across the cafeteria making a beeline straight for the popular kids' table. I don't know why I'm doing this. Maybe part of me feels sorry for Kate that she has to suffer through Brittany's tone-deaf ramblings while she's still obviously grieving the loss of her friend. Or maybe I just need more confirmation that I'm not crazy. Preferably from someone who doesn't have a crush on me and doesn't have a history of agreeing with every single thing I say.

As I approach the end of the table, every person seated there turns their head to face me, each of them wearing near identical expressions of disgust and outright hatred as they land their eyes on me. Even Joel Baker looks annoyed by my presence despite the fact that he was sobbing in my arms just last week. I force myself to turn away from him and direct all of my attention to Kate instead.

"What do *you* want, Liza Lot?" Brittany interrupts her incessant chatter just long enough to sneer at me once she notices my arrival. I feel my cheeks glow red with indignation but I swallow my pride and keep focused on Kate rather than take Brittany's bait like I know she wants.

"Kate, can we talk for a second?" Now it's Kate's turn to start blushing. Her cheeks darken as she pretends not to hear me, but I don't let her ignore me.

"Please," I beg her. "It's important and it'll only take a minute. I promise."

"She doesn't want to talk to you," Brittany snaps. "Why don't you go run back to your little freak show over there and—"

"Shut up, Brittany," Kate interjects before rising from her seat to face me. "This better not take long."

"It won't," I promise, and the two of us walk back to the table where Simon is still seated, leaving Brittany in a state of stunned disbelief as she struggles to locate the precise words she needs to express her outrage. Simon's face is bright red when Kate and I take the empty seats across from him.

"Kate, this is Simon." In a small town like ours, the introduction is unnecessary, but I can't think of anything else to say. There's so much tension between the three of us right now, pleasantries are the only way I can think to dispel the oppressive energy pulsating through the air. Simon whispers a bashful hello and Kate's lips quirk up in a tight smile that looks anything but friendly.

"What do you want from me now, Liza?" Kate huffs. I hate the way my throat constricts when she calls me by that name. It's not like I was expecting our heart-to-heart this morning to change anything, but I was a little hopeful that some progress had been made. Hearing that nickname just makes it official. No matter what history we share, we're not friends, and we'll probably never be friends again.

"Sorry," I mutter. "It's just... I wanted to show you this. Thought you should know."

I push the homework assignment with Mr. Pope's note and the anonymous message from the can of Fix-A-Flat over to Kate and gesture for her to take a look. She doesn't say anything, but she doesn't have to. I can tell from the way her eyes bulge and her brows shoot up to her scalp that she sees the same thing I see. It's not a figment of my imagination. It's not Simon going along with whatever I say. This is real.

Asher is the person who sent us those messages.

"Why are you showing me this?" Kate shoves the papers away like they're contaminated with some sort of flesh-eating disease and they fly over the edge of the table into Simon's lap. He glowers at her before placing them neatly back on the table and folding his hands on top.

"I wanted to get your opinion on it," I reply. "You think the handwriting matches, too, don't you?"

She purses her lips and folds her arms, casting a pair of surly eyes at the ceiling.

"I don't know what to think anymore," she grumbles. At least we agree on one thing. I don't know what to think anymore, either. Still, I need to hear Kate say it. I need to know that she sees it, too.

"Kate, can you please just take another look and—"

"I don't need to look at it again," she snaps. "What do you think I'm blind? I saw it. They match. You happy now? Can I go back to my *friends?*"

Before I have a chance to respond, she pushes her chair back with a loud screech across the linoleum and storms off back to the safety of the popular table. Acid bites at my sternum as my stomach churns in knots, and it's not just because Kate confirmed what I already believed. It was the way she emphasized the word "friends." Like I wasn't one. Like I would never be one. And I know this already. It's been years since we last had anything close to a friendly encounter. So why does it still hurt so much to know that she hates me?

Why can't I just get over it?

"Well, *she's* just lovely, isn't she?" Simon quips, shaking his head as he turns away from watching Kate fall back in line with her *friends*. He sees the hurt in my eyes and grimaces. "You okay, E?"

I shake my head and sit a little taller in my seat, trying not to appear as small as Kate's words made me feel.

"I'm fine," I lie. "Just wanted to know if she saw what we see, you know? Wanted to make sure we weren't freaking ourselves out over nothing."

Simon nods in agreement, but there's a veil of incredulity in his eyes that tells me he doesn't believe me. At least he has the decency not to call me out on it. I don't even want to think about how offended he would be if I told him the truth. That I miss having a girlfriend in my life. That there are some things boys just don't understand, no matter how great of a friend they might be. That even though Simon gives me everything he has, I still somehow need more, and he'll never be able to provide it. Because it's just not the same.

I hate this

"Well, at least you know for sure now," Simon reassures me. "But what are we going to do about it? That's the real question."

I bite my lip and lean back in my chair. This is the part I've been dreading. Even if Mr. Pope is the one who sent the messages and I have the handwriting samples to prove it, that still doesn't help me. It's not like I can go to the cops about it. They'd just ask more questions about why the note was left in the first place. I can just imagine what their response would be after reading those words. *I know what you did.* What did you do, Eliza? And then I'd have to tell them, and before I know it, I'm spending the next however many years of my life in prison.

No. I can't go to the police. Not without incriminating myself in the process. If I'm going to get to the bottom of this, I need to do it on my own.

"I think I need to confront him about it," I decide. Simon almost chokes on the Gatorade he just gulped down, coughing back the urge to spew the blue liquid all over the table as he regains his composure.

"I don't know about that, E." He frowns. "If he really is the one who did this, he could be dangerous."

"Then I'll just need to be careful." I shrug, selecting a French fry from Simon's untouched pile and popping it into my mouth. He groans in response.

"I hate this idea."

"What other choice do I have, Si? If I go to the police, they're just going to ask questions about what the note means. Questions I can't answer unless I want to get in trouble. And there's always a chance that they don't believe me anyway. I mean, you said it yourself. They already think I'm a liar since our stories don't match up."

A flicker of apology flashes across Simon's eyes and I put up my hand, stopping him before he can say the words. "That wasn't a jab at you," I assure him. "I'm not mad.

What's done is done. But I can't go to the police—that's final."

"Fine," he relents. "But I won't let you do this alone. If you're really gonna confront him, at least let me be there with you when you do it."

"Deal," I agree, extending my palm across the table to shake Simon's hand. His shoulders sag with momentary relief before they tighten up again when he realizes the significance behind our handshake.

"So... how are we gonna do this then?" he posits. I bring my thumbnail to my mouth, nibbling at it absentmindedly despite Mom's voice chastising me from somewhere in the ether.

"We need to make sure there are other people around," I suggest. "Honestly, it'd probably be best to just talk to him about it here."

"You wanna accuse a teacher of being a potential *murderer, on school property?*" Simon looks at me like I've completely lost my mind, but I don't flinch.

"Yeah," I tell him. "If we do it here, there's less of a chance that he can lash out at us for it. I mean, this school might be a little—"

"Dinky? Gross? Backwards?" Simon suggests.

"*Dated* was the word I was going to use, but sure. All of the above. Still, there are cameras in the hallways and teachers all over, not to mention the other students hanging around. If we do it here, we'll be protected."

Simon blows out a long, heavy sigh, causing his lips to vibrate as the air passes through them. He leans back in his chair and holds his chin in his hand for a few moments before slapping his palm on the table.

"Screw it," he decides. "We'll do it here. So, when do you wanna do this thing? Should we just head over to his class when school lets out, or is going to an early grave not on your agenda today?"

I roll my eyes and smirk.

"Don't be so dramatic," I tease. "But no. I can't do it today. I have to help my dad at the shop after school. Besides, I think it's safer if we do it while school is still in session. More witnesses around, you know? Just in case."

Simon's throat bobbles as he swallows down his fear.

"So, tomorrow then? After class?"

"Tomorrow," I confirm. Before either of us can come up with an excuse to back out of our plan, the bell rings and lunch is over.

There's no turning back now.

Chapter 21

It's drizzling by the time I park the car in front of Dad's shop, but the raindrops on my windshield are the least of my concerns. Because when I arrive at the general store, my Beetle and Dad's Tacoma aren't the only vehicles stationed in the parking lot. All the muscles in my body stiffen at once.

There's a cop car parked in front of the wraparound porch leading up to Dad's shop.

Again.

Okay, just calm down, Eliza. You knew this was going to happen eventually. I mean, after what Simon told Detective Barnes last night, how could it not? Just take a deep breath (or twenty), shut the engine, and get out of the car.

Do not, I repeat, *do not* try to run away from this situation. You'll only make everything worse.

I finish my pep talk, suck in a lungful of air, kill the ignition, and hopscotch through the parking lot to avoid the puddles gathered between the gravel. As I push through the front door, Riley's howls drown out the sound of the bell chime signaling my arrival. She waddles out from her usual spot behind the counter, wagging her tail as she pads her way to the entrance to greet me. This time, I crouch down and scratch between her ears. Who knows? If this goes poorly, it may be the last time I get the chance to show her how much I love her.

The door to the back-office creaks open and I rise to a standing position as Dad and Detective Barnes filter into the main shop.

Here we go again.

"Hey, honey." Dad's voice is thick with worry despite the smile he forces on his face when he greets me. "How was school?"

I roll my eyes and scoff at the question.

"Really, Dad? *That's* what you wanna talk about right now? Not the fact that a detective is standing behind you?" The smile on his face disappears as his lips peel back into a tight line. I can see his jaw muscles clenching as he grinds his teeth from all the way across the room. Detective

Barnes takes advantage of the silence and steps around him until she's standing in front of the counter with one elbow resting on top as she scrutinizes me.

"It's good to see you again, Eliza," she says. The sweetness in her tone makes my stomach turn sour. It's so fake. We both know she's only here because she thinks I'm a liar. Because I am one. And I'm probably going to have to lie to her again right now. This can't be over soon enough.

"Let's just get this over with," I mumble in response.

"*Eliza*," Dad warns. "Be respectful."

I release the world's biggest sigh and drag my feet along the worn hardwood until I arrive at my dad's side behind the counter. Detective Barnes pulls out her small spiral notebook and equally tiny mini-golf pencil and flicks the pages until she finds the one she's looking for. When she's satisfied, she lifts her eyes in my direction and I swear the deep blue current of her iris is enough to drown me in fear.

"I have a few follow-up questions from yesterday if you don't mind," she begins. I do mind. I mind quite a bit, actually. But she doesn't give me the chance to respond before she hurls the first question at me. "You told me yesterday that you were with Simon Little last Tuesday, is that correct?"

I ball up my fists as tight as I can and give an almost imperceptible nod. Detective Barnes traces a long, thin finger across her notebook until she lands on something that piques her interest.

"You said that you went to his house, spent some time there, and then he drove you home, isn't that right?"

A cold sweat breaks out on the nape of my neck and I shift my weight, already uncomfortable with the way this conversation is going.

"Yes," I admit. "But I—"

"I went to Simon's house yesterday." Detective Barnes cuts me off before I can get another word in. There's an ugly gleam in her eyes when she looks at me. Like when a coyote lurks between the pines, watching from a distance before he finally pounces on his prey. She has me just where she wants me, and she knows it.

"He had a slightly different story to tell me," she continues. "Do you wanna take a guess what it was?"

I don't need to look in Dad's direction to know he's staring at me. I can feel the panic swimming out of his eyes where it splashes against my skin, dousing me with dread.

"E?" His voice crackles with uncertainty when he addresses me. "What is she talking about?"

My knuckles turn white as I clench my fists even tighter, digging my nails into my palm. It's bad enough that Detective Barnes knows I lied. I don't want my dad to think less of me now, too. But I don't have a choice. I have to come clean.

"I didn't do it on purpose," I say, and immediately I regret the words I've chosen. Dad lets out a tiny gasp and Detective Barnes is practically salivating all over the counter as she poises her pencil over the notepad, ready to capture every word of my confession. *Great.* Now they really think I killed her.

"So, it was an accident then?" Detective Barnes presses, her eyes hungry for information. Thirsty for blood.

"Oh my God," Dad breathes, staggering forward to grip the edge of the countertop. I pinch the bridge of my nose and squeeze my eyes shut.

"I didn't *do anything*," I seethe through gritted teeth. "You're not listening to what I'm saying. I meant I didn't *lie* on purpose yesterday. I just *forgot* how things happened."

Dad places a hand over his chest and tilts his head toward the ceiling as though thanking the heavens for not making his daughter a murderer. Detective Barnes is noticeably less enthused by my explanation. The corners of her mouth draw down in a severe frown that ages her ten years before my eyes.

"What do you mean?" she demands. "Explain yourself."

"I'm trying to!" I half shout in frustration. "Look, I was embarrassed, okay? I went to the trailhead to meet up with Carissa and Kate. We got into a fight and things got pretty heated. They tried to beat me up, so I ran away and I left my car at Death Rock. It took me, like, an hour to get to Simon's house on foot. We hung out for a bit, and then it was dark outside, so he drove me to the trailhead so I could get my car. He waited for me to get it started, then I followed him back to my house. That's it."

Detective Barnes taps the pencil impatiently on her notebook and purses her lips. Her eyes narrow on mine like she's trying to look inside my mind to spot the cracks in my story she thinks are still there.

"How much time did you spend at the trailhead when you went back?" I shrug in response to her question.

"I don't know? Like... five minutes tops?"

"Did you see anything unusual when you were there?" A flash of wiry hair and impossibly large limbs lumbering through the forest darts across my eyes and I feel the color drain from my face before I can stop it from happening. I did see something unusual that night, but there's no way Detective Barnes is ever going to believe me if I tell her. But that doesn't matter because she's already seen my response to her question.

She knows I'm hiding something. Again.

"Eliza." She adopts that same sickly-sweet voice that she used the first time she spoke to me. "This will all go a lot smoother if you just tell me the truth."

"Listen to her, honey," Dad encourages me, placing a strong hand on my shoulder. "Remember what I told you? I'm always here for you. I promise."

I take a deep breath and let it out in one long sigh before looking Detective Barnes directly in her sharklike eyes.

"I saw something in the woods," I tell her.

"Something?" She lifts a quizzical brow in my direction.

"Something, someone—I don't know. I didn't get a good look at... whatever it was," I explain. The detective casts a furtive glance at my dad who clears his throat before speaking to me.

"What do you mean, sweetheart?" I lower my gaze to the floor before answering.

"It was while we were driving into the trailhead," I tell them. "I just happened to look out the window, and I saw this... thing walking through the forest."

The quiet that follows is so deafening, for a moment I wonder if I've lost the ability to hear. But then Detective Barnes flips her notebook to an empty page and breaks the silence.

"Can you describe what it is you saw?" I gulp at the question. Of course I can describe it. But I know the instant I do, she's going to think I'm even crazier and more deluded than she already does. I guess that's a chance I'm just going to have to take.

"It was big and scraggly looking," I whisper. "It scared me. When I saw it, I thought it was a... I could've sworn it was a—"

"A Sasquatch?" The mixture of condescension and utter disbelief in Detective Barnes's voice makes me want to scream. She snaps her notebook shut and clucks her tongue against the roof of her mouth, shaking her head as she pockets the pad and pencil. "I think I've heard just about enough of this."

"You asked me what I saw and I told you!" I retort. "*You're* the one who said Sasquatch. Not me."

"Was I wrong?" she shoots back. "Is that not what you thought you saw?"

I open my mouth to respond, then think better of it. There's no point arguing with her. She's already made up her mind. I'm wasting her time, and anything I have to say is just going to make everything worse.

"That's what I thought," Detective Barnes declares, turning on her heel before marching over to the front entrance. As she places her hand on the doorknob, she turns to face me once more. "This is a serious matter, Eliza, I hope you understand that. A girl is dead, and I'm going to find out what happened to her whether you like it or not. Mark my words."

With that, she pushes through the door and leaves me with nothing but the sound of my heartbeat thrumming in my ears.

Crap, crap, crappity crap!

The only way that could have gone any worse is if she hauled me out of the shop in handcuffs. I honestly wouldn't be surprised if she turned around right now and stormed back in so she could take me away to prison. But the anxiety I feel over what Detective Barnes might do to me is nothing compared to the look of disappointment and embarrassment coloring my dad's face right now. He shakes his head in dismay and turns around to head into the back office.

"Dad, I'm telling the truth, I swear," I whine, trailing him from close behind. He sinks into the rolling desk chair beside the ancient computer and rubs his hands over his face. When he resurfaces, there's a strange look in his eyes that I've never seen before. Like even he can't believe what he's about to say.

"I don't want you spending all your time with Simon anymore." My eyes open so wide, they start to water. Or maybe those are just tears because his words have cut me deeper than any hunting knife or Bigfoot claws ever could.

"Dad, that's not fair. You can't do that! It's not his fault!"

"Damnit, Eliza!" Dad's fist comes down hard on the desk beside him and the sound makes me jump. His eyes are wild with anger when he looks at me and it's terrifying. I've never seen him this mad before.

"I am your father and you'll do as I say," he insists. "I don't like what that boy is doing to you. Filling your head with all this nonsense. You're too old for all this now. Detective Barnes is right. This is serious stuff. I won't let you or Simon turn it into one of your little podcast episodes."

I'm so numb, I can't even feel the tears that are streaming down my face and splashing unapologetically to the floor. Is this really my dad? Is this really the same man who spent all last night telling me how he would always be there for me? And now he's ripping away the only friend I have for what? Because I told the truth and he didn't like what he heard? This is so unfair, I don't even have the words to speak. So I don't. I scream instead.

"YOU LIED TO ME!" I holler. "YOU PROMISED I COULD TELL YOU ANYTHING AND YOU LIED TO ME!"

My throat burns from all the yelling and choking, but not as much as my heart stings from the gut-wrenching betrayal I feel. Dad's face crumples and I can see the regret in his eyes, but it's too late.

"Eliza, please. Just calm down. Let's talk about—"

"No!" I yell. "Don't tell me to calm down. I don't want to talk to you. Just leave me alone. I hate you!"

The instant the words leave my mouth, I want to stuff them back in. Especially when I see the agony etched into Dad's eyes like I just reached inside his chest and ripped out his heart. But I don't take it back. I don't say sorry. I don't ask for forgiveness. I spin around and bolt through the door to the main shop, and I don't stop until I'm all the way through the front entrance, back in the safety of Mom's Beetle.

Chapter 22

I barely slept at all last night. The car wouldn't start after the fight with Dad, so instead of driving away to Simon's house like I planned on doing, I spent the afternoon scream-crying in the backseat. Every so often, Dad would come to the shop window making a big show out of adjusting products on one of the front shelves or cleaning the window pane, but I knew he was just doing it to check up on me. It made me feel more than a little guilty knowing that even after saying something so hurtful, he still cared enough about me to make sure I was okay. But then I'd think about why I said what I said in the first place, and I'd get angry and upset all over again.

When it was time to close up the store, Dad dug the jumper cables out of the backseat of his pickup and moved the truck closer to Mom's Beetle so he could give me a boost—all without saying a single word to me. The display on my phone reads seven-thirty A.M., which means it's been fifteen hours since the last time we spoke. I might not have done well on my pre-calculus exam yesterday, but I don't need to be a math wizard to know that this is the longest Dad and I have ever fought in the entire history of our relationship. And I hate it. Because I know that in order for it to end, I'm going to have to be the one to apologize.

Be the bigger person, E, I hear Mom's voice coaxing me out of bed and I have to dig my fingernails into my palms to keep from crying. I know she's right and I know I have to fix this, but there's just something about admitting fault that feels so wrong. Sure, I'll acknowledge that it was wrong of me to tell my dad that I hated him. It was stupid and immature and I didn't mean it at all. But didn't he deserve it just a little? Wasn't it wrong of *him* to forbid me from seeing my only friend? Why am I always the one who has to "be the bigger person?" He's the adult in this situation. Maybe *he* should be the one to apologize first.

I drag my hands down my face and let out a deep groan before swinging my legs over the side of my bed and forcing myself to get up. Sounds of pots and pans and crackling bacon drift in through the crack in my bedroom door, confirming that Dad is also awake. *Great*. Guess I really have to do this. I sigh, pulling a pair of dark blue skinny jeans and an oversized sweatshirt from last year's Bigfoot Festival out of the top drawer of my dresser before scurrying off to the bathroom to get changed, brush my teeth, and splash some cold water on my face. When I finish patting myself dry for the third time, I stop inventing excuses to delay the inevitable and head back to my bedroom to grab my backpack and cell phone before trudging downstairs to the kitchen.

Dad's back is turned to me when I enter the room, but Riley is quick to greet me as she hobbles over from her place lying on the floor beside the dining table, waiting for a tasty treat to fall even though no one is sitting there at the moment. I give her a gentle pat, silently smoothing her coat with my palm while Dad continues cooking over the stovetop, still unaware that I'm in the room with him. As I watch him, I notice things that make me feel even more terrible than I do already. Like how little streaks of silver have sprouted through his chestnut hair, making him look much older and more distinguished than the dad I remember showing me how to cast a fishing line out on South Bay when I was three. Or how the sleeves of his flannel shirt are looking baggier than ever, like one day his muscles just decided he was too old to have them so they disappeared altogether.

It's strange to think of my dad as anything less than invincible. I mean, I'm not stupid. People get old and they die; I know that. Mom died, after all. But Mom was sick and had been for a long time. And after she died, Dad and I were all each other had. In a lot of ways, we still are. So when I look at him now and I see the signs of his mortality staring me right in the face and I hear the echo of the last words I said to him ringing through my ears, I can't help but start to cry. I race across the kitchen and before he has the chance to turn around and identify the source of the booming footsteps sneaking up behind him, I wrap my arms around his waist and bury my head in his back.

"Woah, honey, what's this—"

"I'm sorry, Dad," I croak. "I didn't mean it. I don't hate you. I'm so, so sorry."

Dad lifts his arms above his head and twists around while I cling to him so when he's finished moving, my tears soak through the front of his shirt rather than the back. He grips me by the shoulders and pries me off of him so he can look me in the eyes. His thumbs stroke my tear-stained cheeks as he speaks to me for the first time in what feels like days.

"I'm sorry, too, sweetheart," he says. Then he pulls me back into his arms and holds me against his chest where I remain until the smell of burning bacon forces us apart. Dad curses under his breath and throws the sizzling pan into the sink with a loud clatter before shutting the burner and turning his attention back to me. He twists me around and wraps me in his arms so we're both facing the same direction and I relax my body against his chest, leaning the back of my head into the space just beneath his shoulder.

"I don't wanna fight anymore," I tell him. He lowers his lips and kisses the top of my head.

"It's okay, honey. We all make mistakes sometimes and say things we don't mean. But I love you no matter what. Nothing you say to me will ever change that."

I breathe out a sigh of relief and shut my eyes, happy to be back in Dad's good graces. Then an irresistibly stupid thought enters my mind and before I have the sense to swallow it down, it erupts out of my mouth and ruins everything.

"So, can I still hang out with Simon after school today?" I feel Dad's muscles tighten in response to the question and I already know what his answer is going to be before he speaks the words out loud.

"I don't think that's a good idea." I duck down through his arms and slip out of his grasp, my face blooming red with rage as I spin around to face him.

"But you just said that we all say things we don't mean," I argue.

"Yes, but I meant what I said about Simon yesterday, honey." There's an infuriating calm to Dad's voice that makes me so mad I could spit right here on the kitchen floor. I fold my arms and pout, backing away from him when he tries to pull me in for another hug.

"E, please try to see things from my point of view. You're not even trying to listen to what I'm saying."

"But, Dad, this isn't fair," I whine. "He's the only friend I have and you're just... taking him away from me for no freaking reason! He didn't even *do* anything."

Dad pinches the bridge of his nose and blows out a deep breath before dropping his hand back down to his side.

"Eliza, I know it doesn't seem like it right now, but this is for your own good, okay?"

"How?" I demand. "How could forcing me to be alone possibly be for my own good? You don't think I'm lonely enough as it is without Mom around?"

Tension hums through the air between us as we each absorb the weight of my words. Dad's eyes mist over and his face goes slack with sorrow, like even his skin can't handle living in a world where Mom no longer exists. He swallows hard and the lump in his throat quivers.

"You're right," he whispers, then clears his throat and amplifies his voice. "You're right. You need a friend, and it's not okay for me to take away the one you have. But I still don't like all this Bigfoot nonsense. It's starting to get you into trouble, and I won't have it. So, you can hang out with Simon all you want, but no more podcast. And no more festival. That's final."

"But, Dad, I—"

"E..." The look on Dad's face when he says my name in that warning tone tells me that if I push this any further, I'll be on my way to earning my first grounding. My shoulders sag and I cast my gaze to the floor, allowing defeat to wash over me.

"Fine," I mutter. "No more podcast. No more festival."

"Good girl." Dad reaches over and ruffles my hair before pulling me in for a hug, which I reluctantly accept. "Now, let me whip you up some fresh bacon so I can finish making your sandwich and you can get to school. Should only take a minute. There's still plenty of time before school starts."

With a sullen nod, I shuffle over to the breakfast nook and plop into the nearest chair without even trying to disguise how annoyed and angry I still feel. For all I care,

Dad can take his sweet time making breakfast and earn me my ticket to detention just like Mrs. Morton promised I'd get the next time I show up late to her class. There's no way I can face Simon now. Not with the Bigfoot Festival a week away. Why can't anything just be easy?

I don't have the heart to tell Simon that I can't do the podcast or the Bigfoot Festival with him when I get to school and find him in his usual spot, leaning against my locker. Thankfully, he's too distracted by our plan to ambush Asher Pope after English class that he doesn't even notice how unusually quiet I've been this morning. I guess it's hard to acknowledge someone else's silence when you're too busy talking to hear it. While I'm grateful that Simon's motor mouth keeps him from seeing through my façade, part of me does wish he'd stop talking. The last thing I want to think about right now is confronting a potential murderer.

"We should record it, you know?" The blank expression on my face forces Simon to roll his eyes in exasperation. "The *conversation*, dummy. We should use our phones to record it in secret. This way if he says anything incriminating, we have something to take to the cops."

My stomach flips at the mention of the police, but I do my best to keep my composure so Simon doesn't start asking questions.

"Okay," I agree. "That sounds like a good idea."

"Cool, I'll do it on my phone then." He beams with pride at his clever idea. "Who knows? We might be able to use some of what he says for the podcast. Which reminds me, we *still* haven't done our teaser episode for the festival."

Crap.

We're walking toward the end of the hallway at the junction where we normally split ways to go to our respective homerooms, but Simon's reminder forces me to stop in my tracks. Once he realizes that I've fallen out of step beside him, he spins around and backtracks to where I'm frozen to the floor, unwilling to meet his gaze.

"E, what's wrong?" Simon's forehead is so wrinkled with concern, it reminds me of the ripples on a lake after you skip a stone across its surface.

"Nothing, I... I guess I'm just a little nervous," I lie. Simon's expression smooths over and he slings an arm around my shoulder before we resume walking to the end of the hall.

"I'm nervous, too," he confesses. "But we'll be alright as long as we have each other."

"Thanks, Si." I nestle my head on his shoulder as we walk. "I don't know what I'd do without you."

For the first time all morning, Simon doesn't have anything to say, but somehow his silence speaks volumes—especially when we pull away and I see the look on his face. Like he's dying to tell me something but he's afraid of what my reaction will be. Because the moment he says it, it'll change everything.

I clear my throat to break the tension and shift my weight to my other foot.

"I gotta get to class or Mrs. Morton is gonna give me detention," I tell him. Simon snaps out of his internal debate and plasters the world's fakest smile on his face.

"See you later, E," he says before darting in the opposite direction towards his first class of the day. When he's halfway down the hall, he turns his head over his shoulder and yells, "And don't be nervous! We got this!"

But I am nervous. And the nerves only get worse with every second that brings me closer to Mr. Pope's English class. I don't hear a word of Mrs. Morton's lesson on Kepler's laws. Mr. Phillips might as well be speaking in Latin when he drones on about the Constitution in American Government. When Madame Sage asks me to conjugate the verb *aller* in all six of its forms, I spend an embarrassing five whole minutes at the whiteboard before I finish, and I still get one wrong. I don't even register the fact that I'm in Mr. Atkins's pre-calculus class until the final bell rings and I realize that I've spent the entire period staring out the window. And it looks like I'm not the only one to have noticed my extreme lack of focus. Mr. Atkins is now standing in front of my desk, looking down the length of his perfectly straight nose with this twinge of worry coloring his stare like he's just found a baby bird on the forest floor that fell out of its nest.

"Eliza, can we speak for a moment?" My heart sinks as I anticipate the usual chorus of *ooohs* from my peers, but then I realize that I'm the only one still in the classroom. Everyone else has already moved on to their next class. If I don't leave soon, I'll be late to English, and Simon and I won't have time to make any last-minute changes to our plan.

"I have to get to English," I mutter, gathering up my textbook and sliding it into my backpack as I get up from my desk.

"That's okay," Mr. Atkins assures me. "This won't take long, and I'll give you a note so you don't get in trouble with your teacher."

He flashes a smile full of gleaming white teeth and all the icy walls I've put up seem to melt away in an instant.

"Come to my desk." He gestures for me to follow him to the front of the room, and I oblige. When we arrive at his desk, he takes a seat in his chair and extracts a sheet of paper from the top drawer. "I wanted to talk to you about this."

He slides the paper across his desk for me to see it and my stomach drops to the floor. It's my math test from yesterday, and it's completely blank. I thought that I had at least filled in answers to some of the questions, but the empty paper on the desk seems happy to prove me wrong.

"I've noticed you've been a bit distracted recently," Mr. Atkins observes in a gentle voice and the sound of it brings tears to my eyes. I try to keep them from spilling over my bottom lids, but a few leak out anyway. Mr. Atkins leans forward and grabs a tissue from the box on the corner of his desk which he offers to me.

"Thank you," I whimper. "I'm sorry about the test, Mr. Atkins. I'll try to do better, I promise."

"Hey, there's no need to apologize," he soothes. "I know it's been a difficult week for a lot of students what with the news about Carissa and all. I'm sure a boring math test is the least of your worries right now."

I force a smile as I dab my eyes and thank Mr. Atkins once again for his understanding. Even though he doesn't understand the real reason why Carissa's death has had such an impact on me, it still feels good to have an adult who's on my side for once. Sometimes I feel like he's the only teacher in the whole school who gets what it's like to be a student. He's forgiving, kind, and funny when he gives his lessons, unlike Mrs. Morton and her bone-dry lectures and threats of detention for tardiness.

"I'll tell you what." Mr. Atkins leans back in his chair and stretches his arms behind his head, creating a hammock with his hands where he rests his skull. "Why don't you stay after school on Monday and you can take a make-up test? We'll just forget this one ever happened. Sound good?"

"Oh wow, yes, that sounds perfect. Thank you, Mr. Atkins," I gush. "I'll study real hard for it, I promise."

"I have no doubt you'll ace it." He winks at me and I feel my heart flutter in my chest, but what he says next is enough to bring me to my knees. "And Eliza? You can call me Dave when it's just us. I won't tell."

My face feels like it's on fire I'm blushing so much, but I can't find the words to speak. Mr. Atkins—oops, I mean *Dave*—writes me a note to bring to my next class (which I'm now at least five minutes late for) and when he hands it to me, our fingers touch and I feel like I'm going to pass out.

"I'll see you tomorrow, Eliza," he says.

"See you tomorrow, Mr.—er, I mean, Dave." I scamper out of the room before I have the opportunity to embarrass myself even more. I'm so giddy from the interaction that I don't even remember what it was that had me so distracted in Dave's class until I get to English and I come face-to-face with Asher Pope. He's mid-sentence when I sneak through the door to his classroom and when his eyes land on me, all the panic and dread that I'd been feeling all morning comes rushing back in an instant. I shuffle over to where he's standing and hand him the note before dropping into the empty desk beside Simon.

"Where have you been?" he hisses once I'm settled in my seat. "I was starting to get really worried there for a second. We're still on for—"

"Ms. Loft." Mr. Pope's voice thunders through the room and all the blood drains from my face. "If you're going to be late to my class, the least you can do is get settled quietly. Now, if you don't mind, I'd like to continue with my lesson. Would that be alright with you?"

I cower in my seat and hide behind my hand, feverishly flipping pages in my worn copy of *Ethan Frome* with my free hand until I find what I hope is the correct spot. Mr.

Pope continues talking without waiting for a response to his rhetorical question and I cast a furtive glance in Simon's direction. He mouths "sorry" to me and turns his attention back to the book on his desk. We don't dare to even breathe in each other's direction until the bell rings and class is over.

And now I'm really panicking. Because now I have to do the thing that's been twisting my stomach in knots all day. I have to confront Asher.

Simon and I wait in our seats while the rest of the students filter out of the room. As the classroom empties, Simon takes his phone out and opens the recording app, tapping the big red button at the bottom of the screen before pocketing the device and rising from his seat.

"You ready?"

No, I want to tell him. *I'm not ready.*

Instead, I blow out a sigh and use my breath to propel me out of my desk. Together, Simon and I make our way to the front of the room until we arrive at Mr. Pope's desk. He's busy shuffling through his drawers in search of his car keys so he can leave for his lunch break, so he doesn't notice us standing there right away. Once he realizes that we're there, he hastily closes the drawer and folds his hands on top of his desk.

"Mr. Little, Ms. Loft." He nods to each of us. "Can I help you?"

My mouth goes dry and my hands feel wet and clammy. You'd think with all the time I spent obsessing over this very moment, I would have thought up something to say, but I didn't. So, I just stand there like an idiot while Asher stares me down, his green eyes growing dim with impatience the longer I remain tongue-tied before him. Simon nudges me in the ribs, snapping me out of my trance. He raises his eyebrows at me expectantly, urging me to speak.

"I... I need to talk to you," I finally say. My heart is pounding so loud in my ears, I barely hear it when Asher asks, "About what?" It seems he's not the only one growing annoyed with my cowardice because Simon seizes the opportunity to answer for me when I fail to produce the words.

"About why you left that note in her locker," he blurts. "We know it was you. Show him, E."

My arms feel like they're made of rubber as I slide the backpack off my shoulder and start to dig around in my bag for the handwriting samples I still have tucked inside. But before I can lay them across Asher's desk to gauge his reaction, he stops me.

"That won't be necessary," he says. He rises from his seat and I swear to God I feel like I'm going to pee right where

I stand. As he towers over us, it's the first time I appreciate how truly massive he is. It's not just his height. He's got these broad shoulders and bulging muscles that look like they're going to burst through the seams of his dress shirt. Even though he's only five years older than either of us, the sheer size of him makes me feel like I'm a toddler in his presence. This was a mistake. Bigfoot or not, this guy could crush us both in an instant if he wanted to. And something in his eyes tells me that he wants to.

Asher begins to walk around his desk and Simon grabs me by the shoulder, shoving me behind him to act as my human shield.

"Stay away from her!" he commands. Asher halts in his tracks and throws his hands up in defense.

"I'm not going to hurt you," he assures us. "I... I'm sorry."

"Sorry for what?" Simon pushes. "We want to hear you say it. Admit it right now!"

Asher drops his hands to his sides. His face goes slack as his lips form a tight, thin line. The three seconds he takes to collect his thoughts feels like three years, and when he finally speaks, the earth shifts beneath my feet.

"Okay," he says. "I admit it. I put the note in your locker."

"*And* Kate's, *and* Carrisa's," Simon reminds him, and Asher nods.

"Yes," he agrees. "I did it. It was wrong, and I'm sorry."

"Oh yeah? If you were really sorry, then you wouldn't have killed Carissa," Simon retorts. Asher's brows pull together and a flicker of fear dances through the forest in his eyes.

"Wait a minute," he stammers. "That didn't happen. I didn't touch Carissa."

"Yeah right," Simon bites back. "Why send a threat if you weren't gonna follow through on it? Admit it. You killed Carissa because you thought she, Kate, and E knew about your dirty, little secret."

"Oh?" The fear is gone from Asher's eyes now and is replaced with something far more menacing. "And what secret is that exactly? Enlighten me."

"That you killed your sister in the woods that night." As the words leave Simon's lips, I can almost pinpoint the instant they reach Asher's ears from the way he staggers backward and his eyes go dark. His nostrils flare, and for a moment, I think he might wrap his hands around Simon's neck and start squeezing. Instead, he speaks in a low, steady growl.

"I didn't *touch* Renée," he seethes. "And I didn't touch Carissa, either. You don't know what you're talking about."

Simon opens his mouth to respond, but I interject before he can get another word out and make Asher even angrier than he is already.

"Why did you put the notes in our locker if you weren't trying to threaten us?"

Asher rakes a hand over his face and steps back toward the whiteboard, gripping the ledge as he steadies himself against its surface. I tug on Simon's shirt sleeve and make a gesture for him to keep his mouth shut and wait for Asher to speak first. We don't have to wait for very long before he launches into an explanation.

"It wasn't meant to be a threat," he says. "I was just... my sister meant the world to me. We were best friends growing up. We did everything together. Fishing, hiking, swimming—you name it, she was there with me doing it. Then I went away to college, and I don't even get through the first semester before I get the call that she was... that someone..."

He sinks his head into his hands and his shoulders begin to shake. Simon and I are too shocked to say anything. It's not every day you witness your teacher have a complete emotional breakdown right before your eyes. Asher wipes his face with his sleeve and sniffs, sucking in a shaky breath before continuing.

"I'm sorry," he croaks. "I just miss her so much. I know it's ridiculous, but I felt responsible somehow. Like if I had just been there to protect her, none of this would've happened. And what made it even worse was the fact that no one could figure out who did it. They found her tires slashed up and her broken little body, but they couldn't find the person who took her away from me. So, I decided I was gonna find them myself.

"I couldn't find out very much. The cops are pretty tight-lipped about open cases. But I started hearing these rumors around town about how Renée's tires got slashed." Asher looks over at me and smirks at the horrified expression I can feel stretched across my face. "Don't act so surprised," he says. "It's a small town. People talk."

"But we promised to never say anything about it," I counter.

"Like I said—people talk," he replies. "I was at a buddy's house for a party and Carissa just happened to be there, trying to fit in with the older crowd. She had a few drinks and started running her mouth about some stunt she pulled when she was a kid with her friends in the woods. No one else knew what she was talking about. She was pretty vague about it and most of us were wasted, but I knew.

"It didn't take me long to figure out who her friends were in the woods that night. Again, small town. Everyone knows who everyone else hangs out with, even if they haven't in a long time. So, when I got the job at the high school, I decided to try and scare you all a bit. See if one of you would start feeling guilty enough about what you did to come clean. The janitor's an old friend, so I just made up some excuse about needing to get inside and he lent me the keys to do what I needed to do."

"Wait a minute," I interrupt. "The cops always thought that whoever slashed the tires was the same person responsible for Renée's death. Did you think that we...?"

"At first, yeah," Asher admits. "I thought maybe the three of you were trying to cover up for something more than just the tires. But after thinking about it more, it just didn't seem plausible for you all to have done it. When they found Renée, she was... no. It wasn't possible for you to have done that to her. But I thought that maybe one of you saw something that night while you were out messing around, and if I scared you enough, maybe you'd be willing to talk about it. And maybe it would help me find whoever did this to my sister."

Simon and I exchange a nervous glance, but neither of us has the courage to speak. It doesn't matter, though, because Asher isn't stupid. He can see the unspoken words written across our anxious faces more clearly than he would have heard them if we had uttered them aloud.

"You did see something that night, didn't you?" he asks. "Please, tell me what it was. I need to know what you saw. I need to find who did this. It's... it's killing me inside."

I sink my teeth into my bottom lip and let my shoulders sag. If I tell Asher what Simon and I think we saw in the woods that night, he's just going to have the same reaction that Detective Barnes had in the shop yesterday. But I can't let him go on like this. Even though he's kind of creepy and I still don't entirely trust him, I recognize the look that's in his eyes. It's the same look I had when Mom was lying on her deathbed. The look that tells anyone who can see it that you'd do anything in the world just to stop the hurt inside. I wouldn't wish that kind of torment on anyone—not even the person who left a terrifying message in my locker just to scare me.

"Look, we'll tell you what we saw, but not here," I relent. "It's too much to explain, and you won't believe us if we try."

"Okay... so where do you want to talk about it then?" Asher raises a quizzical brow and I dart my eyes at Simon, silently apologizing for what I'm about to suggest.

"Can you meet us at the Bigfoot Museum after school lets out?"

"*E, what are you doing?*" Simon hisses. I elbow him in the ribs to shut him up and Asher takes a step forward with his open palm stretched out for a handshake. I place my hand in his and he gives a firm shake.

"Deal," he says. "I'll drop by around four o'clock."

Chapter 23

We're sitting in the back office of the Bigfoot Museum and Simon hasn't stopped pouting since we got here. He's sitting on top of the computer desk with his arms folded and his brows scrunched together like a toddler who refuses to eat his vegetables while I pace around the tiny room, actively avoiding his gaze. I understand why he's annoyed; I probably should have consulted with him first before extending an invitation for Asher to meet us here. But what else was I supposed to do?

"This is stupid," Simon grumbles. "You didn't even ask me first. He could be lying about everything!"

"Look, I know you're mad at me, but we don't have any other options, Si," I tell him. "He wouldn't have listened to us if we just told him what we saw. He'd just jump to conclusions before we even got the chance to tell him everything else."

"Oh yeah? And what makes you so sure about that?" I pause mid-step as I realize that I still haven't told Simon anything about what happened at my dad's shop yesterday. He notices my hesitation and doesn't give me the opportunity to debate whether or not I should tell him.

"What's wrong? Did something happen?"

Crap.

Why does he have to do that? Why does he have to know me so well?

"Yeah, something happened," I admit. "The detective came back to the shop yesterday."

Simon's eyes widen and he unfolds his arms so he can grip the edge of the desk to steady himself.

"What did she say?"

"Just that she knew that I lied about not going back to the trailhead." I put up a hand to stop the apology before it has a chance to leave Simon's lips. "Then she asked me whether or not I saw anything unusual while we were there."

"And? What did you tell her?"

"I told her the truth." I recount everything that I said to Detective Barnes and Simon listens without interrupting. "When she asked me to describe what I saw, I told her, and she completely shut down. Accused me of not taking this seriously and basically said she was gonna make it her mission to find out what happened whether I liked it or not. Like she still thinks I'm involved or something!"

"She said that?" Simon lets out a low whistle and shakes his head, and I see the wave of understanding start to crash over him. I nod and take a seat in the rolling desk chair.

"So, do you get it now? If we just told Asher what we saw, he would've just stopped listening to us before we got the chance to tell him everything else we know," I reiterate. "At least if he's here in the museum, we can show him the message board posts. Plus, your parents are out front so it's not like he can hurt us or anything while they're around. Just in case."

Simon nods silently. He knows I'm right. But neither one of us wants to acknowledge what I mean by "just in case." Even if we did, we wouldn't have gotten the chance because no sooner do the words leave my lips than we hear the distinct sound of a Sasquatch call signaling Asher's arrival as he walks through the front door.

"Oh, Asher! What a pleasant surprise." I hear Mrs. Little's sing-song greeting through the closed office door. "What brings you into the museum today? Not that I'm not thrilled you're here. It's just... I've never seen you at the festival or anything. Didn't peg you as a believer."

Simon and I file out of the back room to join his parents and Asher at the reception desk. It's a little strange seeing him outside of school, but it's even weirder to see him standing next to the cardboard cutout of a Sasquatch in the middle of the Littles' Bigfoot Museum. Simon's mom is right to ask questions. Asher doesn't fit the stereotypical mold of a Sasquatch believer with his khaki pants and neatly tucked dress shirt.

"I'm here to see Simon and Eliza, actually," he responds in a polite voice, looking past Mrs. Little's narrow shoulder until his gaze lands on me and Simon. I give an awkward wave in return.

"Oh, how nice," Mrs. Little comments with a smile. "Are you helping them out with the podcast?"

"Something like that," I interrupt before Asher has the chance to verbalize the confusion written all over his face. "We're all set up in the back room if you wanna join us."

Asher presses his lips together and gives me a curt nod before excusing himself from Simon's parents with a gracious smile. Simon and I head back to the office and Asher follows in our footsteps until the three of us are packed into the small space like a can of worms waiting to be speared onto a fishing hook.

"So, you were going to tell me what you saw." Asher wastes no time getting to the point.

I can tell from the strained expression on his face that our earlier conversation has been haunting him all day. The way he's looking at us right now is the same way my dad looked at the oncologists when they first gave us Mom's diagnosis. Like we somehow hold all the answers. Like there's a chance what we have to say could change everything for the better. I clear my throat and gesture for Asher to take a seat while Simon takes his usual spot, hopping up on the computer desk.

"Before we tell you what we saw, I need to tell you what we did first," I begin. My pulse is thrumming so hard through my veins, I feel like they might burst open. I wipe my sweaty palms across my jeans and take a deep breath. "You said you overheard Carissa talking about what we did to Renée's car, but she was vague. I want to tell you exactly what happened."

"E, you don't have to—"

"It's okay." I cut Simon off before he can finish. "He already knows some of it. He deserves to know it all."

Asher straightens in the chair and waits for me to speak. His eyes are like tree sap oozing from the trunks at Aunt Josie's maple farm, sticking to my skin as he watches me struggle to locate the words I need to tell him the secret that's been gnawing at my soul since the night it happened. But once I find them, they tumble out of my mouth in one, long breath. I tell him all about what happened to Mom, how angry and rebellious I had been after she left me. I tell him about all the times that I'd sneak out with my Dad's bottle of whiskey so Carissa, Kate, and I could get wasted in the woods. I tell him all about the game of Truth or Dare. I tell him everything. And I don't look at him a single time until I'm finished.

When I dare to glance in his direction, I expect him to be angry or hostile or full of contempt. Instead, he just looks sad. No, not sad. It's deeper than that. Like he wasn't just listening to my story. He was *living* it. Like my guilt is his guilt, and for the first time since he showed up at Whitehall High, when I look at him, I see him for exactly who he is. He's not a vindictive, scary, psychopathic teacher with a grudge. Standing this close to him in the museum's cramped little closet of an office space, I realize that Asher isn't even that much older than us. In a lot of ways, he's just as much of a kid as we are. A kid that feels responsible for something he can't change, but wishes with everything inside him that he could. A kid just like me.

"I know it doesn't change anything, but you have to believe me when I say that I really didn't know it was Renée's car," I tell him. Asher swallows hard and nods, swiping his sleeve over his face to absorb the tears he thinks I can't see in his eyes.

"I know you didn't," he whispers. "Thank you for telling me the truth."

"That's not the full story," I continue. "After we slashed the tires, I was too drunk to ride my bike home, so I had to walk it back all by myself through the woods. I didn't make it very far before I started hearing noises coming from the forest."

"Noises?" Asher lifts a brow as if inviting me to clarify and I gulp.

"Screams," I answer finally. "I thought it might have been Carissa or Kate at first since they took off before me. So, I went to go see if they needed help, and that's when I saw it."

"Saw what?" I cast a nervous glance at Simon before answering Asher's question. This is the moment I've been dreading. He'll either take off running and assume the worst like Detective Barnes, or he'll stick around long enough to hear the entire story. There's only one way to find out.

Here goes nothing.

"I saw this... thing attacking your sister," I say. "It was big and hairy and stood up on two legs. I'd never seen anything like it before. Not outside of the festival anyway."

I watch the realization morph across Asher's face as he digests what I've just told him. He looks from me to Simon, then back again, and I can tell he's trying to decide whether or not we're totally insane.

"Are you telling me that you guys think a Sasquatch killed Renée?"

"Not exactly," I answer, but my response is contradicted by Simon's simultaneous reply.

"Yes," he says. I snap my head in his direction and throw my hands to the sky.

"What the heck, Si?" I demand. "That's not what we decided."

"Speak for yourself," he retorts. "I know what I saw, and so do you. It's not my fault you don't want to believe your own eyes. Heck, you even saw it out there *again* the night Carissa died."

"Simon..." I cover my face in my hands, mortified by my friend's outburst. Now Asher is definitely going to think we're crazy. The whole point of bringing him here was to try and gain his trust, but Simon just threw that possibility right out the window. I'm certain that when I uncover my hands from my face, Asher will be out the door. But when I finally drop my hands at my sides, my English teacher is still sitting in the rolling desk chair, a look of deep contemplation on his face. I'm surprised to see he hasn't left, but what he says next shocks me to my core.

"What makes you so sure it was a Sasquatch?" It's not the question he asks so much as it is the way he delivers it. Like he's genuinely curious. Like maybe a small part of him believes that it could be the truth. Simon clears his throat and sits a bit taller on the computer desk, like he's a hip, young professor eager to launch into an expert oration on the topic of cryptozoology.

"Well, for starters, it looked just like one," he states matter-of-factly.

"How do you know what they look like? It's not like there are any clear pictures of them."

Oh brother. That was the wrong thing to say. I don't even need to look at Simon to know his face has turned crimson and his back has gone rigid and he's about to go on a tirade of epic proportions. It's the same thing that happens whenever a skeptic shows up at the Bigfoot Festival and starts raising questions about the validity of the folklore our little town holds so dear. I just breathe out a sigh, select a corner of the wall to lean against, and listen to the storm of facts and figures I've heard a million times before.

"Pictures? *Pictures?*" Simon scoffs and shakes his head. "Pictures don't mean squat. Did you know that the African Golden Cat was first described in 1827, but the species was so elusive that no one could get a *picture* of it until 2002? *And* they didn't get video of it until ten years later. So, I ask you Mr. Pope, did the African Golden Cat not exist before 2002? Were all the scientists and explorers who had ever seen it up until that point just delusional morons? Or are you more willing to believe in a cat's existence because it's a cat, and it doesn't force you to think about the fact that only forty-two percent of the entire world has been explored and there may still be things out there that we have yet to discover?

"I'll have you know that there have been over three hundred reported sightings in the Adirondacks alone since 1819. And Native American tribes have passed down stories of the *Sasq'ets*—supernatural shapeshifters and protectors of the land—for hundreds of years. Are they just making it up? How many different accounts from different cultures all reporting the same exact thing do you need before you have to admit that *we* aren't the crazy ones. *You* are."

Simon ends his spiel with a huff, giving Asher this self-righteous smirk like he's just daring him to make a counterargument. But Asher doesn't give him the satisfaction. He just puts up his palms in defense and bows his head in defeat.

"Alright, alright," he says. "Fair enough. It just seems a little... unbelievable is all. I mean, you have to admit, it's a big leap to make. A *Sasquatch* attacked my sister? It doesn't make sense."

"Oh, but believing she was killed for no reason by some random psycho does?" Simon challenges. "You said it yourself. This is a small town and people talk. I haven't heard anything about Renée or Carissa having any enemies serious enough that they would resort to murder—have you?"

Simon waits for a response, and Asher just shakes his head. Then they both turn to me, and I wish that I could melt into the wall. Because unlike them, I have heard rumors about a potential motive—at least for Carissa. But it's only after hearing Simon declare that no such motive exists that I realize I'm the only one in the room who has this information. Ever since I discovered the match between Asher's handwriting and the mysterious note in my locker, I had all but forgotten about what Kate told me. What Simon still doesn't know. And the way he's looking at me now, like he can see right through me, I know he's not going to let me get away with staying quiet. So, I don't even try. I just come right out with it.

"I think you're wrong about that, Si," I tell him. "You're forgetting about the message board posts. But besides that, there's—"

"Wait, what message board posts?" Asher interjects before I get the chance to finish my thought. Simon rolls his eyes and snorts.

"Here, I'll show you," he mumbles. He slides off the computer desk and brings the machine to life so he can pull up the forum. Asher rolls the chair closer to the screen once Simon gives him the okay to take a closer look. As he reads, a deep frown forms a crease in his face, making him look like an old man.

"Have you shown these to anyone?" he asks and we shake our heads in reply.

"We didn't think anyone would believe us," I say. "But the posts match up with when Renée died *and* when Carissa died. And—"

"Wait, what about this one?" Asher interrupts me for a second time before I'm able to get the words out. He points an index finger to the second post in the sequence—the one dated July 20, 2023. I had almost forgotten about that post and it dawns on me that I was so distracted by the connection to Renée and Carissa that I never took the time to read what it says. Leaning over Asher's shoulder, I gaze into the screen to read the message:

> **reelbigfoot19:** The monster was in Saranac Lake. A pretty little camper gone for a

late-night swim. He fileted her like a fish on
the shore. No one heard her screaming. But
I did. I saw the whole thing. And it won't
be the last time. Because I'm always on the
hunt.

"Is there another victim we don't know about?" Asher prompts after I finish reading, but I'm too frozen with fear to respond. After Carissa died, the Saranac incident completely skipped my mind. But as I read the message on the board, I'm more convinced than ever that I'm right.

It's not a Sasquatch committing these attacks. It's a person.

Simon takes a quick look at the message and leans against the desk, rubbing the back of his neck with a slight look of embarrassment on his face. Even he can't deny that this kills his theory about Bigfoot, but he's not eager to admit it.

"Forgot about Saranac," he mutters. "Yeah, a girl died over the summer. One of the campers. No one found out who did it, but a few other people on the board witnessed it too and they all said it looked like it could have been a Sasquatch."

"But what if it wasn't?" I whisper, and everyone's eyes turn to me. I swallow hard, choosing my next words carefully. "What if it's this reelbigfoot person pretending to be one?"

"You think someone's out there masquerading as a Sasquatch?" From the tone of his voice, I can tell Asher finds this somehow even more far-fetched than he already found Simon's "Bigfoot exists" argument. But I keep talking anyway.

"I don't think they're doing it on purpose," I explain. "But I do think they're taking advantage. Read what it says. *I'm always on the hunt.* What if that's true? What if they *are* hunting? Hunting people. Hunting *girls*. Maybe they wear a ghillie suit when they do it. That way they're disguised. And if anyone does catch them in the act, it wouldn't matter, because all they would see is what we saw. All they would think is—"

"Bigfoot." Asher completes my thought and the three of us let the realization settle. Not even Simon can think of a way to spin this back in favor of his Sasquatch theory. A long silence passes before Asher finally clears his throat and turns his attention to me. "You were going to say something earlier. Before I cut you off."

My cheeks glow red and I cast my gaze to the floor.

"Yeah, I... I know something you guys don't," I confess. "Simon, you said before that there wasn't a motive, but I don't think that's true. Not in Carissa's case, at least."

"What do you mean?" His brows twist together like twin serpents across his forehead.

"Kate told me that Carissa was having an affair," I blurt out. "She didn't tell me who with, but it sounded to me like it was an older guy. Not a student in the school. What if this older guy is the one who's been doing this? What if he's, like... targeting young girls or something? I don't know."

When I look at Simon, his eyes are wild with astonishment. If he shakes his head too hard, they might just fall right out of his skull, he's that floored by what I've just told him. Then I turn to Asher, and my stomach hardens with ice. All the color has drained from his face. His green eyes make me seasick from the way they don't sit still, like he's reading the subtitles on one of Madame Sage's French films but the words are moving too fast. Suddenly he clears his throat and stands up so fast, the chair almost topples over.

"I just remembered I have to be somewhere," he murmurs before fleeing from the room like the walls are burning down around him. I don't even have time to register the fact that he's gone before I hear the Sasquatch call telling me that he's already left the building.

"What the heck was that about?" Simon demands, his eyes still fixed on the open office door. My mind drifts back to that day at the soccer field as Kate's confession skips around in my skull like a broken record. *She was having an affair.* I don't know how to respond to Simon's question, but I do know one thing.

Asher still can't be trusted.

Chapter 24

I've had that nightmare every night since the day we met with Asher at the Bigfoot Museum. But instead of an impossibly huge, hairy beast sitting in the driver's seat, it's Asher's face buried behind a mossy ghillie suit. It's his glowing red eyes boring into me, daring me to make a move. And when I do, it's his claws digging into my abdomen. His hands pulling out my intestines until I wake up gasping for breath, wondering if I'll ever have a good night's sleep again.

Simon and I haven't gotten the chance to hang out since the day it happened. Even though he swears up and down that I'm allowed to be friends with him, Dad keeps inventing excuses for me to have to help him at the shop so I can't go off to Simon's house over the weekend. So, that's where

I end up all Friday afternoon and all day Saturday and Sunday. Even today I'm supposed to head in for another shift (like the shop is suddenly a mega mall in the heart of Albany or something), but Dad agrees that I can come in a bit late after I tell him that I have to stay after school to work on a project. I don't mention that the "project" is me making up a math test that I failed because I was too busy trying to figure out who the monster is that's terrorizing the girls in Whitehall. If I tell him that, there's a very strong possibility that I'll never get to see Simon again. And I can't have that. Not when we're so close to finding out the truth.

The final bell of the day rings and as I exit Mr. Marvin's home economics class, I bump into Simon on my way to take the makeup exam.

"Hey, can you come by the museum later?" I frown in response and shake my head.

"Sorry," I tell him. "I can't today. I have to go to D—to Mr. Atkins's class to take a makeup test, and then I have to go straight to the shop."

"Again?" Simon groans and rolls his eyes. "You were there all weekend, and we *still* haven't done a podcast episode. The festival is Saturday, E. If we don't get an episode out before then—"

"I know, I know." I sink my teeth into my bottom lip. "Look, I don't know if I'm gonna be able to swing it this week, Si. My dad's been really on me lately to be at the shop. Do you think you could maybe just... do it solo? Just this once?"

"*What?* Are you kidding? We're supposed to be a team. We're supposed to—"

"I'm sorry, okay? But I promise I'll make it up to you," I tell him. "I'll find a new guest for the live show. How's that?"

Oh my God. Why did I say that? I'm such an idiot. There's no way I'll be able to follow through on that promise. But it's too late now because Simon is already throwing his arms around me like I'm the messiah come down from the heavens to tell everyone that Bigfoot really does exist. Why did I have to go and open my big mouth?

"Thanks, E. I really appreciate it," he croons in my ear as he holds me to his chest. "I tried reaching out to the Saranac posters on Friday, but they said it was too short notice to do it. And with all the prep for the festival I still need to do with my parents, I just don't have the time to find a guest."

"No problem," I mumble back. But it is a problem. It's a huge freaking problem that I don't have an answer to, and I'd better come up with one quick or it won't matter that

Dad is actively trying to keep me away from Simon because he won't want anything to do with me anymore anyway once he realizes that I'm full of crap. Simon releases me and the grin on his face makes me feel even grimier than I do for lying to him. Again.

"I'll see you tomorrow," he says. "Thanks again!"

And before I can go back on my promise, he takes off down the hallway toward the bus loop to catch a ride back to his house, leaving me standing in the throng of students all clambering to escape the prison that's held them captive since eight o'clock this morning. But not me. I still have a warden to answer to. A very cool, very attractive warden who insists on me calling him by his first name.

Get a grip, Eliza.

By the time I make it through the doors of Dave's classroom, the stream of students in the hallway has thinned to a steady trickle with just a few stragglers taking their time as they chat with friends and prepare for the short walk home. As I enter, Dave stands up from his desk and straightens his tie.

"Good to see you, Eliza." He smiles and I feel the heat rise in my cheeks. How is it that such a small gesture can turn me into a complete bumbling idiot every time I see it? He takes a sheet of paper off his desk and waves it in the air. "Ready for a do-over?"

"As ready as I'll ever be." I shrug and take my usual seat in the middle of the room. Before I have the chance to sit down, Dave stops me.

"Why don't you sit closer to me?" he suggests, motioning toward the seat in front of his desk. If he didn't notice me blushing before, it's impossible to ignore now. I can feel my pulse in my face, my cheeks are burning so red. As I sink into the chair he selected, he approaches my side and pats me on the shoulder.

"Good girl," he murmurs. Between the sexy purr of his voice and the warmth radiating from his hand as he squeezes my shoulder, I feel like I'm going to melt into a puddle right on the floor. He places the paper down on my desk and glides over to take a seat behind his.

"You have forty minutes to complete the test starting... now. Best of luck."

I bow my head to the desk and get to work on the exam, grateful for a reason to avoid Dave's piercing blue eyes that make me feel like I'm floating in the crystal pools at the bottom of Carver Falls on a hot summer day. Still, I can't seem to focus on the questions on the page. Once again, I'm distracted, only this time it's not my personal drama that's keeping me from getting any work done. It's the fact that any time I lift my gaze from the page in front of me, I catch Dave staring at me and my heart skips several beats before it finally finds its rhythm. How do any of the girls in school make it through his class without failing?

Before I know it, forty minutes is up and I have to hand in my work. Even though I'm sure that I answered about ten of the questions incorrectly, I'm happy that I at least provided an answer to every single one. That alone will be enough to keep my grades from slipping into oblivion.

I bend down to grab my backpack off the floor and when I go to stand up, Dave is sitting on top of my desk with a beguiling grin tugging at his lips. If I didn't know better, I'd think he was flirting with me. But then I remember that I'm seventeen and Dave is a grown man with absolutely zero interest in a teenage girl, and even if he was, I wouldn't be his type. With his perfectly cropped blonde hair and chiseled jaw, he'd probably prefer a cheerleader if he was going to make the career-ending decision to get involved with a student. In my baggy Bigfoot Festival tee shirt and acid-wash jeans, I'm far from the image of perfection that belongs on Dave's arm. And even though I know this is all just a fantasy in my extremely hormonal, totally screwed-up head, for some reason the realization still hurts.

"How do you think you did?" Dave's voice pulls me out of my internal torment and I force the unclean thoughts away so I can at least pretend to have a rational discussion.

"I, uh... think I did okay, I guess," I stammer. Dave chuckles and slides off my desk, and I seize the opportunity to stand while my knees still feel strong enough to support me.

"Well, we'll see soon enough." He winks at me (God that wink). "You still seemed distracted though. I was watching you as you worked. You seem preoccupied with something. Is there anything you'd like to talk about?"

Just the fact that I think you're totally gorgeous.

I force the inappropriate response from my mind and swallow down the words before they have a chance to explode out of my mouth.

"No, I'm okay. Really," I tell him. He clucks his tongue and shakes his head.

"C'mon, Eliza, I'm not that dumb," he insists. "You can trust me. If there's something bothering you, I want to help. That's what I'm here for, aren't I?"

He takes a step forward so there's only about six inches of space separating us. He's so close, I can smell his aftershave, and the scent of pine and wood mingling in my nostrils makes me feel as high as Aunt Josie after she gets done smoking a joint filled with the homegrown marijuana in her "secret greenhouse" she thinks I don't know about. I can tell Dave isn't going to let this go, so I just say the first thing I can think of that doesn't involve me confessing my schoolgirl crush.

"I guess I'm just stressed because the festival is this week and Simon and I are supposed to do a live podcast episode, but we still don't have a guest for the show."

There. That's not a lie. And it seems to do the trick because Dave's face relaxes and the concern in his eyes disappears.

"You know, I'd be willing to help you out with that if you want," he offers, and I almost fall over from disbelief.

"Wait, really?" I splutter. "Why would you do that?"

The instant the words leave my lips, I feel like an ungrateful idiot. *Really, Eliza? You couldn't just say thank you?* But Dave doesn't seem to take offense. He just laughs it off and flashes one of his heart-attack-inducing grins before responding in an easy voice.

"I know I don't seem the type, but I'm actually quite fond of the Sasquatch lore in our little town," he confesses. "Besides, I like you, Eliza. Your family has always been so accommodating to me at the shop. Helping you with your show is the least I can do to repay you."

"Wow, I... I don't know what to say," I falter. "Thank you so much. Simon is going to be so relieved."

"It's my pleasure," he assures me, and I have to consciously coach myself not to swoon. As I float down the hallway out to the student parking lot, my thumbs fly over my cell phone screen as I type out an excited message to Simon.

> **Monday, October 2, 3:50 p.m.:**
> I found a guest for the live show and you're never going to believe who it is!

Chapter 25

Just as I thought, Simon was ecstatic when I told him about Dave's willingness to be on the live show at the festival. All week long, he's been singing my praises, gushing about how this is the perfect opportunity to bridge the divide between believers and skeptics.

"Think about it, E." He slings an arm around my shoulder as we walk through the crowd of students making a mad dash out the door to get a head start on the weekend. "Everyone in school respects Mr. Atkins. When they hear that even *he* believes in bigfoot, everyone's gonna lose their minds. It'll be pandemonium! The museum will be overflowing with visitors. Mom and Dad are gonna flip. God, you are a genius. I could just..."

He catches himself before he completes the thought and clears his throat, unraveling his arm from around my shoulder. I pretend not to notice the trail of red creeping up his neck to his chin as he holds the door open for me and we step out to the student parking lot. It's Friday—the last day before the festival tomorrow—and we're planning on doing a practice run of the live interview with Dave later this evening. But first, Dad insists on me making an appearance at the shop. He doesn't know that I still plan on doing the podcast and the festival. I'm sure he'll figure it out tomorrow when I'm gone all afternoon and into the night, but for now, I'm happy to avoid another fight by omitting the truth.

As Simon and I approach the end of the overhang that juts out from the school's front entrance and step into the sun, he glances at the bus loop and does a double-take.

"Oh *crap!*" he yells as he watches the doors to his ride home snap shut and the bus driver pulls away from the curb. He takes off running before he can say a proper goodbye, hollering over his shoulder at me instead, "See you later, E! Can't wait!"

I shake my head at him and laugh to myself as I walk over to Mom's Beetle at the far end of the parking lot closest to the football field where the cheerleaders are busy practicing on the sidelines. At the head of the pack, I can see Kate's unmistakable curls bouncing on top of her head as she twirls through her routine. It looks as though she's taken Carissa's spot as the captain, and I have to admit, she's completely in her element as she pops, locks, and poses in perfect rhythm with her fellow cheerleaders. I take a moment to stand and watch. Even though it's not my scene and even though I know she still hates me, I can't help but feel a surge of pride seeing her step into her role as the leader of the group. It suits her.

In the middle of her routine, Kate catches me staring and the two of us lock eyes. She nods at me with her chin as if to say, *Hey*, and I lift my hand to wave. I know it's not the same as us being friends and it will probably never go back to the way it was when we were kids, but somehow it still feels good. Like it's the start of something new. Like maybe there's hope that one day, we will be friends again. And when that day comes, I'll be ready—whenever that might be.

I feel my phone vibrate through my jeans and lift it out of my pocket to find a text from Dad.

> **Friday, October 6, 2:44 p.m.:** You're still coming to the shop right?

Ugh. Yes, Dad. It's been ten whole minutes since the bell rang. Take a chill pill!

Instead of texting any of that, I type out a quick message that I'm on my way and turn around to head back to the car. I slide into the driver's seat, drop my backpack on the passenger's side, stick my key into the ignition, twist, and... nothing. Not even the angry whine of an engine that wants to work but can't. So, I take the keys out, pop them back in, and try again.

Still nothing.

Even when I try a third time, feathering the gas pedal as I attempt to start the car just like Dad taught me to do when it acts up this bad, I don't get the smallest hint of mechanical activity working its way through the vehicle. On the fourth try when nothing happens, I slam my fist into the center of the steering wheel and curse. I finally have to admit to myself that it's done. The car is dead. Just like the person who owned it.

I know it's stupid and it shouldn't upset me this much and to everyone else, it's just a car, but to me, it's just one more piece of my mom that's gone forever. One more thing I can't control. One more disappointment stacked up in a giant mountain of disappointments that's been piling up on my shoulders since the day Asher Pope showed up in my English class. So, I can't help it. I fold my arms over the steering wheel, sink my head into my makeshift cocoon, and I cry. I'm crying so hard and so loud that I don't even hear the knocking on my window at first until I lift my head up to catch my breath and I see Dave staring down at me on the other side of the glass.

Oh my God!

This is hands down the most embarrassing moment of my entire life. Here I am, throwing a tantrum in my car like some loser, and the hottest guy I have ever seen just happens to catch me in the act? The same one who I'm supposed to interview for a podcast later? All of a sudden, I'm not angry or upset at the car anymore. I'm jealous of it. Because I want to be dead, too.

I dab my face on my sleeve and hoist myself out of the car, and I reluctantly face my math teacher, still choking back tears. The friendly grin on his face is replaced with a look of grave concern as he assesses me. For some reason, seeing him look at me like that sends me over the edge, and before I can stop myself, I break down crying all over again.

"Hey, hey, shhh." Dave folds me into his arms and lets me sob into his shirt, stroking my hair as he holds me. "It's okay, Eliza. I'm here. Tell me what happened."

"It's–s–s my M–m–mom's c–c–car," I stutter through my tears. "It won't st–t–tart."

"Oh, honey, is that all?" he soothes. "Don't worry. I can take you where you need to go."

I pull away and peer up at him as a fresh tear glides down my cheek.

"Really?" I whimper. "You'd do that?"

He lifts his hand and tucks a strand of hair behind my ear before wiping away the stray tear with his thumb, and his touch makes me shudder. I know he doesn't mean anything by it other than to be nice to a suffering student, but somehow it feels more significant. And the look in his eyes when he stares into mine only makes me feel even more enamored with him. Like maybe I'm not imagining this. Maybe he really does find me attractive. Me. Eliza Loft. Complete laughingstock of the entire school. Bigfoot believer extraordinaire. Can't even get her own car to start. Somehow this perfect man is looking at me like I'm the most beautiful creature he's ever laid eyes upon, even as my face is soaked with saltwater.

"Come with me," he murmurs. And I don't hesitate for a second. I dart around to the passenger's seat and lift my backpack out of the Beetle before I follow Dave to his car at the opposite end of the parking lot where all of the teachers park their vehicles. As we walk, I cast a longing gaze over my shoulder at Mom's car. Even though I'm thrilled at the prospect of spending extra time alone with Dave, I feel a pang of regret sting my heart when I see the unmoving station wagon. Before I turn back around to face forward, I catch Kate staring back at me. She's too far away for me to see the look on her face, but she's waving at me and the sight of it makes me smile despite myself. I wave back to her before turning away, continuing the journey to Dave's car with a slight bounce in my step. Mom's car might be toast, but it looks like my friendship with Kate really is being resurrected. At least something is working out in my favor—for once.

Dave opens the passenger side door to his dark blue Honda Accord and I blush as I slide inside the vehicle. *He's such a gentleman.* How is it possible that there's even a small chance he might be into me? I shake the thought from my head before it has time to take root. It's so messed up. It doesn't matter how handsome or polite or kind he is. He's my freaking teacher, for crying out loud. Who does that? No one, that's who. Just keep your mouth shut, get to the shop, and thank him for the ride when you get there. Don't be a freak.

My internal dialogue ends when Dave climbs into the driver's seat, inserts the keys to the ignition, twists, and the engine comes immediately to life. Just like it's supposed to happen. Like it's not something he has to pray for every time he wants to go somewhere. *Lucky.*

"So, where're we headed?" he asks.

"I have to go to the shop," I tell him, and he gives me another one of his winks that makes my heart balloon in my chest.

"Your wish is my command," he says. And before I know it, we're pulling out of the parking lot and onto the main road. It's quiet in the cabin and I can't tell if it's the awkward silence or the disorientation of being in an unfamiliar car, but I get the strangest sense of déjà vu as we ride through town together. Like part of me feels as though I've been in this exact situation before, but I can't put my finger on why. I'm about to mention it to Dave just to break through the quiet, but the moment I open my mouth to speak, my phone rings and the sound of it is so loud that I jump in my seat.

That's odd.

I must have toggled it off silent mode when I answered Dad's text before. But that's not even the weird part. When I take the phone out of my pocket, there's a strange number displayed across the screen that I don't recognize. Rather than answer it, I hit the button to send the caller straight to voicemail. As I place the phone back in my pocket, I look up just in time to see that Dave has driven straight past Dad's shop.

"Hey," I blurt. "You just passed the store."

"Oh... did I?" There's an odd tone in his voice when he answers. Like he's mocking me or something. The sound of it sends an icy chill down my spine.

Don't panic, Eliza, I tell myself. *It was just a mistake. Everyone makes mistakes. Just like Dad said.*

But then Dave misses his opportunity to turn around at the next street.

And the next.

And the next.

And suddenly I realize that it wasn't a mistake at all. My pulse quickens as I try to think of something to say, but before the words enter my mind, my phone rings again. When I remove it from my pocket, that same number from before is displayed across the screen. This time, I don't hesitate to answer.

"Hello?"

"Eliza, it's Kate." I'm so shocked by the sound of Kate's voice that I almost drop the phone out of my hands.

"Kate? But how did you—"

"I never got rid of your number," she interrupts quickly. "Listen to me, are you with Mr. Atkins right now?"

I dart a nervous glance at Dave and watch him turn his head in my direction. My heart leaps to my throat.

"Eliza, answer me. Are you with Mr. Atkins?" Kate's voice is frantic when she repeats the question and I stumble over the words as they flood to my mouth.

"Yes, yes—why?"

"Shit," Kate hisses in my ear. "Eliza, you need to get away from him now."

I clench the phone tight against the side of my face and brace myself for the answer to the question I'm about to ask.

"Why?"

"Remember how I told you that Carissa was having an affair?" My throat constricts and my vision blurs at the edges. "Mr. Atkins was the guy she was seeing. I've been thinking about it ever since we talked, and I think you're right. I think he's the one who—"

"Okay, that's quite enough of that, don't you think?" Dave snatches the phone out of my hand and smashes his thumb down on the "End" button, terminating the call with Kate. Then he slides the phone into his pocket before placing his hand on my knee.

"Oh, Eliza." He tuts and shakes his head. "What have you done?"

And that's when I realize why I've been having déjà vu since the moment I climbed into Dave's car. Because I *have* lived this before. Over and over again, almost every night since the night Renée died. I'm stuck in my nightmare with no way out.

And Dave is the monster that's going to kill me.

Chapter 26

I've never been this scared in my entire life, and even though I've had the dream enough times to know exactly what comes next, I still can't wrap my mind around the fact that it's happening. Like part of me thinks that this really is a nightmare and I'll wake up before the scary part. But this isn't a nightmare. This is real life. I can tell from the way Dave's hand pinches my knee as he clamps down on it with his hand and I don't wake up. A pinch is always supposed to wake you up from a bad dream—isn't it?

Dave drives past the edge of town, deep into the winding dirt roads of West Mountain. The forest is so thick, it doesn't even matter that the sun still has at least another hour left until it dips below the horizon. It might as well be the middle of the night from the way the tall pines loom overhead and block out whatever light remains in the sky.

"I used to bring her here, you know? And Death Rock," he tells me like I want to make conversation with him. Like I'm not terrified by the mere sound of his voice. "Carissa, I mean. And Renée. Those two couldn't wait for the chance to be alone with me. They'd be so jealous of you right now."

For the first time since he took my phone away, he removes his hand from my knee and uses it to caress my face. An hour ago, a gesture like that would've made my heart beat out of my chest with desire. Now it just makes me feel like I'm going to vomit. He slides his hand under my chin and forces me to look at him.

"You really are so beautiful, Eliza," he tells me. "Do you know that? I've noticed you for a long time. But Carissa, well... you know how she was. So eager. So *willing*. How could I resist that? But you? You're different than her. Because you don't even realize how gorgeous you are. And that's what makes you special, honey. That's what makes me want you even more."

His hand snakes its way around the back of my neck and he pulls me into him, forcing me to rest my head on his shoulder while he continues to drive deeper into the woods. I'm paralyzed with fear as his words rattle around in my skull, and it's all so confusing. Even though I know that everything he's saying is a lie, there's a tiny seed of insecurity planted deep inside me that feels satiated by his compliments. And that somehow makes me feel dirtier and more pathetic than the feel of his thumb tracing circles on the nape of my neck as he drives.

With each stroke of his thumb, a fresh trail of goosebumps rivulets down my spine and pools in the pit of my stomach until it churns with acid and the bitter taste of bile bites at the back of my throat. My body quivers and before I know it, I'm choking on tears as they dribble down my chin and spill onto Dave's lap.

"Oh, honey, don't cry," he croons. "You're so much prettier when you don't cry. This is supposed to be fun. There's no reason to get upset."

"Wh–where are w–we g–going?" I whimper.

"You'll see soon enough," he replies, and the sinister edge in his voice makes my ears ring. "I used to go hunting back here a lot growing up. Lots of great game around these parts. Turkey, deer, coyotes even—you name it, I killed it. But you know, it gets old after a while. I mean, where's the fun in killing something that can't even really *think* for itself? There's no challenge in that. There's no sport. It's just cruel. But people? Well... that's something else entirely."

Before I can stop myself, I let out a shriek so ear-splitting that it feels like flames might burst out of my mouth and the car windows might shatter from the sheer volume. But Dave just laughs like it's the most pleasant sound he's ever heard.

"Go ahead and scream," he encourages. "I love a good scream. Here, I'll join you."

He rolls down the window and puts his head through the opening as the car continues careening through the darkened trees that surround us. With the breeze blowing through his blonde locks, he unhinges his jaw and unleashes a bone-chilling scream of his own. When it's over, he brings his head back into the cabin and rolls up the window. An evil glint flashes in his eyes when he looks at me.

"No one will hear you scream," he assures me. And the moment he says it, I feel my heart stop. Because I've heard that phrase before. Well, I didn't *hear* it.

But I read it.

"Y–you're... you're reelbigfoot19."

"*Very* good, Eliza." He slings his arm around my shoulders, holding me even closer to him as he drives. "You're the only one who put that together. I guess that's no surprise, though. Only a true believer like yourself would be caught dead in that stupid forum. People are so gullible.

Especially in this town. Everyone's just looking for an excuse to claim they saw a Sasquatch. So pathetic. Works in my favor, though, so you won't hear me complaining. Why do you think I have the ghillie suit? It's not just for camouflage. If anyone catches me in the act, they'll just think it was Bigfoot. You of all people should know that."

He winks at me, and my mouth falls open.

"H–how did you—"

"I've listened to your podcast," he says. "What? You don't think I enjoy a good show? I'm one of your biggest fans, Eliza. You and Simon have done wonders to help keep my extracurriculars under the radar. The way you two talk about Sasquatch encounters, you might think they actually *do* exist."

My stomach lurches and I feel myself gag. Dave sees me struggling and unhooks his arm from around my neck, shoving me away.

"Don't you dare throw up in this car," he warns. "The last thing I need is your DNA all over the damn interior. Just hang on. We're here now anyway."

I look through the windshield and watch as the pines open up to a small clearing. Dave swerves the car to the right and parks it, and I waste no time throwing the door open and spilling out into the darkness. I cough a few times before the vomit pours out of my mouth and splashes at my feet. As I grip my knees and try to catch my breath, I hear the trunk of the car slam shut behind me. I straighten to a standing position and spin around. The shadows make it hard to see clearly, but when my eyes land on Dave, I don't have to guess what the deflated pile of mossy-looking material is that he has gathered in his arms.

He shakes out the ghillie suit like a blanket and finds the opening before stepping inside and zipping it over his clothes. I'm so stunned, I can't think of anything to do but stand and watch as he steps around the car and approaches me.

"Are you ready to play?" he asks. I stumble backward and catch myself on the hood of his trunk.

"Wh–what do you mean?" I don't want to know the answer, but it's all I can think to say. Dave takes a step closer and wraps his moss-covered hand around my wrist, pulling me closer to him. He lowers his head so that his eyes are level with mine and he speaks in a low growl.

"I want you to run, Eliza."

My teeth begin to chatter and my knees quake. I dart my head from side to side, desperate to find an escape, but all that surrounds me are trees, trees, and more trees. He wants me to run, but there's nowhere *to* run. There's nowhere to hide. There's no point in even screaming. All I can do is squeeze my eyes shut and pray that God will somehow grant me mercy. Please God, I know I've told you countless times how much I miss my mom, but I'm not ready to see her just yet. I'm so young. There's so much I still want to do. There's so much I still need to see. I've never even had a boyfriend. I've never even been kissed. Oh God. I don't want to die. I don't want to die. I don't want to—

The sound of police sirens cuts through my thoughts and I swear, I almost pass out from the relief that rains down on me.

"Whitehall PD!" An authoritative voice calls through the air. "Put your hands where I can see them!"

I spin around to face the source of the voice and stupidly put my hands in the air like I'm the one in trouble. Dave seizes the opportunity to grab me from behind and pull me into his arms. I scream and thrash and kick his shins, but his grip only gets tighter the harder I struggle to break free. Then I see a flash of silver glint in his hand before he brings a blade to my throat, and all I can do is surrender because I know any sudden movement will just end up getting me stabbed.

"If you come any closer, I'll kill her!" Dave hollers.

"DROP YOUR WEAPON!" The cop shouts back. Dave drags me a step backward, attempting to disappear into the trees. I watch the officer step closer to the end of the vehicle, and as the flashing lights dance across her face, I realize that it's Detective Barnes. "I SAID DROP YOUR WEAPON!"

"And I said don't come closer," Dave growls. And before I know what's happening, I feel this intense pressure in the pit of my abdomen as the knife slides into my intestines. The pain is so excruciating, I don't even realize that I'm screaming until my knees hit the ground and the sound of my shrieks is replaced by a deafening blast. The last thing I see before the world goes black is Dave's body falling to the forest floor and the red lights from the police car reflected in his irises as the life drains from his eyes.

Chapter 27

I wake up to the smell of iodine and bleach. There's a funny taste in my mouth and my throat feels dry and sticky when I swallow. Loud beeping noises drift into my ears along with softspoken voices murmuring somewhere in the distance. I blink a few times before my vision clears and I see that I'm in a hospital room. As I try to sit up to get a better look around and grab someone's attention, the pain in my stomach takes my breath away and I collapse back into the bed.

"E, honey, don't move." Dad places a warm hand on mine and gives it a gentle squeeze. He tosses his head over his shoulder toward the open door to the hospital room and calls out for a nurse. A few moments pass, and a petite brunette with square-framed glasses glides into the room, followed by Detective Barnes.

"You gave us quite the scare there, kiddo." The nurse scrunches her nose as she beams down at me and I groan in response. "I'll bet you're in a lot of pain. Let me adjust your medication."

She fiddles with the machine beside my bed that I only just realize is connected to an IV in my arm. When she's finished, I hear a click and a warm, fuzzy feeling starts in the crook of my elbow before it travels through my veins, covering every inch of my body until the pain is nothing but a pinprick of pressure somewhere above my belly button.

"That should do it." The nurse winks at me, and I wish I had the strength to hug her. But I don't, so I just say thank you instead. "No need to thank me, honey. I'm just doing my job."

She nods at my dad and Detective Barnes, then darts from the room to give us some privacy. Detective Barnes takes a step forward and clears her throat.

"It's good to see you again, Eliza," she says. Only this time when she says it, I can tell she means it. And maybe it's the drugs coursing through my veins, but boy is it good to see her, too. She grabs an empty chair from beside the door and drags it to the side of my bed next to Dad.

"I know you're still in a lot of pain and you're probably not up for it right now, but I'll need a statement from you about everything that happened tonight once you're healed."

At first, I don't understand what she's talking about. But then the memories come rushing back to me. The car. The phone call. The monster.

I shudder.

"Is he... dead?" I croak. Detective Barnes and Dad share a look, but this time my dad speaks before she gets the chance.

"He's gone, honey." He sniffs. "He won't hurt you again."

I shut my eyes and breathe out a long, shaky breath as the tears trickle out from my eyes. But I'm not crying because I'm sad that Dave is dead or because the pain in my stomach is still sharp enough to make it hurt to sob. I'm crying because I'm so relieved. I'm alive. I'm safe. I'm innocent.

It's over. It's finally over.

Detective Barnes places her hand on my knee and I have to fight the urge to jerk it away. Even though I know he's gone, I can't get the memory of Dave's hand on my knee out of my mind. It's too fresh. But I let the detective keep it there because I know she's not going to hurt me. For once, she's on my side.

"Eliza, I just wanted to say that I'm... I'm sorry," she says. "You tried to tell me the truth, and I didn't listen to you when I should have. I know nothing I say will ever make that right, but I just wanted you to know from the bottom of my heart and on behalf of the entire Whitehall PD, I am very, truly sorry."

The corners of my mouth curl up in a faint smile and a few more tears sneak their way down my cheeks.

"It's okay," I tell her. "Everyone makes mistakes sometimes."

Detective Barnes pats my knee once before taking her hand away. She scoots back from the bed and rises from her seat, but before she can head through the door, I stop her.

"Can I ask you something?"

"Anything you like," she answers.

"How did you know where to find me?"

Now it's her turn to smile at me. "Let's just say you have some very smart, very caring friends," she replies. My brows bunch together in confusion, so she elaborates.

"After Ms. Richards called you, she went straight to the museum. I guess she was hoping that she'd find you there. When she arrived there, she explained what was happening to Mr. Little and both of them came straight to the police. We had already been looking into Mr. Atkins after a tip came in from another teacher at the school last week, but we didn't have much else to go on. Once Ms. Richards told us about the affair between him and Carissa and the fact that he abducted you, we knew we needed to act fast."

Oh my God. So, that's why Asher left the museum so abruptly last week. He wasn't having an affair with Carissa after all. But something still isn't making sense to me.

"I don't get it," I tell her. "That still doesn't explain how you—"

"It was Simon who found you, Eliza," she interjects "Apparently, you had a Share My Location feature switched on your phone. If it weren't for his quick thinking, I don't know that we'd be having this conversation right now."

With that, she tips her hat and exits through the door.

Holy crap. Simon saved my life. Again. And Kate helped him do it. Maybe we really are friends, after all. As though reading my mind, I see a tuft of curly hair accompanied by a dark woman adorned in brightly-colored clothing and my eyes just about fall out of my head.

"*Kate?*"

"Eliza!" Kate rushes into the room and grabs my hand. "Oh my God, I've been so worried about you. When I saw you following Mr. Atkins, I just knew something was wrong and I tried so hard to get your attention before you left but you didn't stop and I—"

"Slow down." I giggle, and the laughter makes me grimace from the pain. Kate rips her hand away from mine.

"Oh no!" she gasps. "Did I hurt you?"

"No, I just... don't make me laugh so much maybe." I smirk. She breathes a sigh of relief and wraps her hand around mine. We stay like that for a moment before Mrs. Richards cuts through the quiet.

"Eliza, I'm glad to see you are well." She gives a curt nod, and I know it's the closest thing that I'm going to get to an apology from the woman who shooed me off her front porch like I was nothing but a no-good criminal trying to corrupt her daughter's innocence. I nod in return, and Mrs. Richards turns her attention to my dad. "Mr. Loft, would you care to join me for a coffee? I think these girls have some catching up to do."

Dad looks at me with anxious eyes, but I tell him it's fine. I'm okay. For once, I really am okay. He gets up and follows Mrs. Richards out the door, leaving me and Kate in the room alone. She sinks into the seat that my dad just abandoned and bites her lip.

"E, I... I'm really sorry," she whispers. "I was so mean to you for so long, and even though I'd like to say it was all

Carissa's fault, I know it wasn't. I could've been better. I *should've* been better. But I—"

"You called me E," I interrupt.

"Yeah, I... I hope that's okay," she says, sheepishly tucking a strand of hair behind her ear.

"Does it mean we're friends again?" I ask. She shifts in her seat.

"If you wanna be," she answers.

"Then yeah," I tell her. "It's more than okay."

She breaks out into a wide grin that somehow travels through the few feet of space that separate us and finds itself mirrored on my face. I notice a few tears slide down her cheek, but I don't mention it because I can feel them gliding down my own as well. And just like that, we're friends again. Like nothing ever happened. She opens her mouth to speak, but as soon as she does, we both snap our heads toward the hallway through the open door as the sound of thunderous footsteps pounds through the air. Ten seconds later, Simon is standing in the doorway, gasping for air.

"E!" he yells. "Oh my God, E. Oh, I'm so glad you're alive. I didn't think I'd ever see you again. I thought I lost you forever. I thought—"

"I'm right here, Si," I assure him. "And I have you to thank for that. Both of you. Really. Detective Barnes told me everything. If it weren't for the two of you, who knows what would've happened?"

The three of us exchange a meaningful look, and even though none of us says a word, we don't have to. Because in this moment, we know that there's no doubt about it. We're bonded for life. And I couldn't be happier to belong to such a wonderful group of friends.

Simon steps into the room and gives Kate this pleading look. She nods in response and gets up from her chair, then gives me a warm smile.

"I'm gonna go get a snack from the vending machine," she says. "I'll be right back."

As she passes Simon on her way out the door, she gives him a thumbs-up sign that she thinks I can't see. It seems that in their fight to save my life, these two have become closer than I ever thought imaginable. They even have secret signals now. What the heck is that about?

Simon doesn't waste time occupying the chair that Kate left behind. He slides it closer to the bed and slips his hand in mine.

"Are you in pain?" He grimaces.

"A little," I answer. "Where're your parents?"

"Oh, they're around." He shrugs. "I think they went with your dad and Kate's mom to grab a cup of coffee before coming up here."

I nod and before I get the chance to say anything more, Simon beats me to the punch.

"E, I have to tell you something," he says. "And I don't care if it ruins everything. I don't care if you never want to speak to me again. Because tonight made me realize that this life is too short to keep things bottled up inside, and I can't keep this from you anymore. So, here goes... E, I—"

"I know, Si," I tell him. And as soon as the words leave my lips, his face flushes pink. He reaches his free hand behind his neck and rubs.

"It's that obvious, huh?" he groans. "How long have you known?"

"A while," I answer.

"And you weren't gonna say anything?" I giggle in response. The look of complete mortification on Simon's face is just too funny.

"I was waiting for *you* to say it," I tell him. He smirks, and the color in his cheeks deepens. His hand starts to tremble around mine, and I see his knee shaking as he taps his foot up and down, up and down, up and down. "What're you thinking?"

He hesitates a moment and bites his lip, as though debating whether or not he's going to say what I know he's wanted to say since the moment he walked through the door. But instead, he surprises us both.

"Screw it," he mutters. And before I know what's happening, he rises from his seat, leans over the edge of the bed, cups my head in his hand, and he kisses me. His lips are so soft against mine, they feel like clouds, and when he pulls away, it's like he takes the entire sky with him. He leans his forehead against mine, peering into my eyes as we share a smile, like neither of us can believe what just happened. And even though the wound in my gut makes it hurt, this time, I like it when the butterflies scrape against my stomach lining. So, I let him do it again.

THE END

About the Author

K.T. Carlisle is the pseudonym for a nomadic writer located in the United States. Since early childhood, Carlisle has dedicated her life to the written word. Earning her B.A. in Writing Arts with a concentration in Creative Writing in 2015 from Rowan University, Carlisle received the Excellence in Writing Arts award from the university—an honor reserved for students who exhibit exceptional skill as a writer and teacher of writing.

When she is not busy working on her next novel, Carlisle spends her days exploring the U.S. in her travel trailer with her three crazy dogs. For more information, or to inquire about rights, permissions, speaking engagements, and more please visit www.ktcarlisle.com.

Acknowledgements

To my sister, Sara, thank you for your constant belief in me and my stories. Your encouragement and enthusiasm give me the courage to keep writing, even when I feel like giving up. I love you more than words can possibly express.

To my father, John, thank you for always believing in me and pushing me to pursue my dream of being a published author. I'm sorry that you weren't here to see my dream come true, but I hope that wherever you are, I've made you proud.

And finally, to you, dear reader. Of all the countless books you could have selected, you chose this one. Without you, none of this would be possible. Thank you from the bottom of my heart for taking this journey with me. I hope it is the first of many we will share together.

Printed in Great Britain
by Amazon